HONOR

DIVINE DEITIES

RYE BREWER

CHAPTER 1

Most storylines are predictable.

Most storylines have a villain, a victim, and a clear distinction between the two. Villains are almost always obviously bad. They do immoral things and treat everyone around them poorly. In contrast, the victim is usually the opposite of that—the singular stroke of goodness that seeks to overcome their oppressor. There is never any confusion between them; the power dynamics are clear.

Life isn't like that.

I can't remember when I learned that. It seems like a fact of life that I was born accepting as truth, the way that I know the sky is blue and the grass is green. While everyone else around me sought to see the world as clearly black and white, I saw things in shades of gray.

We aren't all good or all bad. I'd like to think that I try to be a decent person more often than not, but that doesn't mean I haven't considered being cruel many times throughout my life.

Even now, as I walk down the aisle to marry an immortal prince of Hell, it's unclear if I'm the victim or the villain of my own story. I was forced to go to the Underworld by my father, the god named Zoren, and marry Prince Elijah of the kingdom of Disgrace in exchange for the King of Hell's assistance in helping my father earn back the kingdom he lost from the goddess of deceit. This was never my plan, even though Elijah is reasonably nice and mild-mannered. Thus, you'd think that I was the victim.

However, it's not as easy as that. First of all, I'm not in love with Elijah. He's tolerable, especially in comparison to his other brothers, but I don't love him the way a wife should love her husband. And yet, I'm willingly walking toward an altar to make a lifelong promise based on the assumption that I do feel that way about him. Isn't that immoral? Wouldn't I be lying?

When I say *lifelong promise*, I mean it. As a demigoddess, I'm expected to live about twice as long as a regular mortal, but marriage to a prince of Hell means that I'll eventually be made immortal. I will literally live forever. I'll be married to Prince Elijah forever. And ever.

And ever.

Of course, there was never an expectation that any of my father's daughters would fall in love with the God of the Underworld's sons. The marriages were arranged, first and foremost, for a political alliance. Did that let me off the hook?

Leave it to me to be waxing philosophical on my own wedding day. Growing up, when my mother wasn't too busy throwing suspicious glances at the twins and their mother in Zoren's palace, she was chastising me for spending too much time with my nose in a book. Every time she did so, I gently reminded her that she was the one who decided to procreate with the god of arts and literature. My odd habits were at least partially her fault.

But maybe my mother had a point. She was in the mortal realm now, living in one of the horribly polluted human cities that you only heard nightmarish stories about, and I was never going to see her again… but I knew what she'd be saying to me if she was in the Underworld on my wedding day.

"Not everything is a puzzle of logic to solve,

Chloe," she would say. "Sometimes things just are the way they are. Try to live in the moment."

That was easier said than done.

Still, I did my best.

The traditional marriage procession music was trilling throughout the grand hall. Architecture in the Underworld favored marble and other nearly impenetrable stone as materials, especially in darker hues. Because of that, I was getting married in a large room with a vaulted ceiling, seemingly held aloft by thick columns of deep blue marble. A thousand yellow candles gleamed, their reflections glowing like stars in the glossy medium.

I was wearing white. In most kingdoms, no one would bat an eye at such a thing, but in Hell, very few people wore such light hues. Two weeks ago, my older sister Riven got married in a gown so dark it was as if it was made from the shadows itself. The train of her dress trailed several feet behind her, flowing like an inky stream down her back and onto the floor.

Riven liked melodrama. I did not.

When the God of the Underworld announced that he wanted to speed up the marriages, there wasn't much planning needed for mine and Elijah's union. We were both fairly casual people. I wore a white dress, and he wore his traditional princely regalia in tones of deep gray. The ceremony was far less elaborate and sensational than Riven and Prince Finn's wedding, but that was the way I preferred it.

I wasn't a huge fan of being in the spotlight.

I could tell Elijah didn't like it either. He waited for me at the altar with a timid gaze, the lightest color of pink in his cheeks hinting that he would give anything to get rid of the hundreds of eyes trained on him at that moment. I wished I could walk faster, but my steps had to match the pace of the slower-than-death tempo of the music.

Elijah looked like his brothers for the most part, at least until you saw him up close. From a distance, the six sons of the God of the Underworld all appeared to be tall, broad-shouldered and possessed dark hair and eyes. However, there were differences between them that had nothing to do with their varying ages. Prince Elijah, the third son, had subtle auburn undertones in his dark hair... perhaps a trait he inherited from his mother, who had scarlet hair and ruby eyes to match the Red River she created and claimed as her domain. Also, while Finn and Nico had black eyes, Elijah's were lighter—almost hazel.

He was handsome, of course. Anyone with eyes

and a brain could acknowledge that. But there were other things in life besides romance and handsome men. I wasn't opposed to doing my duty and fulfilling my father's order to marry Elijah, but I wasn't doing it in the hopes that I would experience heart-stopping love.

In truth, I saw it as a once-in-a-lifetime opportunity to have access to incredibly vast wealth of research and knowledge that existed in the Underworld. It was one of the oldest and most powerful kingdoms known to all. Some of the greatest minds came to the Underworld over the millennia hoping to impress the King of Hell with their intellect.

On top of that, it's not like it was a bad thing to have a husband, especially one as influential as Prince Elijah. I was twenty years old, so I was expected to find a suitable match soon anyway. Marrying Elijah would provide me with financial stability, a roof over my head, and all the books I could dream of getting my hands on.

So, really, things could be worse.

But things weren't perfect. My eldest sister Rose hadn't been thrilled to learn about the arrangement our father made with the God of the Underworld; she had a difficult time fitting into her new life with Prince Finn and ended up running away with a servant boy. Now her lover was dead—executed by the God of the Underworld—and Rose was suffering in the darkest pits of Hell for the next fifty years.

Of course, her twin Riven was quick to swoop in and snatch the eldest prince, the heir to the throne of the Underworld, in Rose's absence, leaving her former fiancé Prince Nico high and dry.

But that wasn't what I wanted to be thinking about on my wedding day.

Finally, I reached the end of the aisle and placed my hands in Elijah's waiting palms. I took a deep breath and took my spot opposite him, the God of the Underworld stood between us with a calm, impossible-to-read expression on his face. I'd learned that's just how the ancient god was. It was difficult to figure out what he was thinking or feeling, but at least you would know for certain if he was upset. The entire world trembled when the King of Hell was angry.

Elijah and I shared a glance. I felt as nervous and uncomfortable as he looked, itching under the quiet stares of the audience on either side of the aisle. It was a smaller crowd than Riven and Finn's wedding, but only slightly.

The God of the Underworld cleared his throat,

and then his voice boomed throughout the room, echoing off the cathedralesque ceiling.

"We have gathered here today to witness the union of my son, Prince Nico of the kingdom of Disgrace, and the third daughter of Zoren, demigoddess Chloe," he began. "They will be bound for eternity in unholy matrimony…"

The rest of his speech was a blur. All I could focus on was keeping my legs from trembling and trying not to appear too anxious. Elijah held my gaze the entire time, and it began to feel like that was the only thing keeping me upright. When he said his vows, his voice was impressively clear and stable, so I did my best to match him so that I didn't look like a complete fool in front of the most important people in the Underworld.

"I do," I said at last.

"I now pronounce you husband and wife, Prince and Princess of Disgrace," announced the God of the Underworld.

Elijah leaned forward to press a chaste kiss to my cheek as the room exploded with applause. We clasped hands and turned to face them.

Prince Finn and Riven were the first people I noticed, both clapping with restrained, close-lipped smiles. Beside them was Prince Nico of Corruption, newly single thanks to Riven's stunt, and with no word of a new partner to replace her. He looked as though the last place he wanted to be was at another wedding, especially if it meant he was forced to sit beside Riven and pretend he didn't mind that she wasn't his anymore. I didn't blame him for his visible displeasure. Honestly, I felt bad for him.

Riven had always been difficult to predict, but one thing was for certain—she would always take the route that served her interests above anyone else's before she stooped to accept anything less than what she wanted.

Elijah led me back down the aisle, nervous smiles plastered on both of our faces. The ceremony melted seamlessly into the reception.

"Please remind me that I'd never again like to be the guest of honor at a single event for the rest of eternity," Elijah murmured in my ear as we stood in the center of the ballroom and prepared to perform our first dance as a married couple.

"Happy to do it," I replied, avoiding Riven's amused smirk as she watched me take Elijah's hand and wait for the music to begin with blushing cheeks.

"In fact, I've recently been considering becoming a hermit," Elijah continued, his voice low in my ear as we began to step in time to the music, our cheeks a mere inch apart.

"A hermit's life sounds lovely to me," I whispered.

"It's settled then," he said. "We will build a wall around the kingdom of Disgrace, and we shall never leave. In time, they will forget we existed in the first place, and we'll be blissfully left alone for the rest of eternity."

He was joking, of course. Elijah didn't speak much, but I learned over the past few months that his humor was based on nearly imperceptible sarcasm. Most of the time, those around him didn't even know that he was kidding when he cracked a joke which, in my eyes, made it even funnier.

The first night we met, mere hours after I parted ways with my father and my sisters to take a carriage to Disgrace and begin my new life, I sat at dinner with the stranger I was engaged to and tried to understand his nuanced expressions.

There was a lady at the court of Disgrace named Veronica, the half-mortal daughter of a duke and a nymph who lived with Raya in the Red River, who obviously hoped that *she* would be the one to earn Elijah's hand in marriage. I was very good at reading people. When you consume as much literature as I have in the span of twenty years, there are very few things people can do that will surprise you. Veronica was obvious like that, her bared-teeth smile when she curtsied to me and her clipped commentary on the "ever so unexpected" nature of our betrothal told me everything I needed to know.

Thankfully, it was also clear that Elijah didn't entertain her affections.

At the dinner table on that first night, Veronica let out a loud sigh and playfully slouched in her chair as she preened her elaborate curls.

"What a truly magnificent evening," she murmured, leaning halfway across my lap to get closer to Elijah at the head of the table. "I wanted to make sure I dressed perfectly for the occasion, but can you believe that it took me nearly four hours to get ready for dinner tonight?"

Veronica wore a ridiculously fanciful gown that glittered with tiny onyx stones—which was hardly a subtle choice at all—and had on so much makeup on her admittedly pretty face that I swore it was as if she were trying to put on a mask.

Elijah looked at her for a long second.

"Yes," he quipped.

Confused, Veronica sat back in her chair. She'd expected Elijah to politely lie and say that her entire ensemble appeared beautifully effortless—that was the acceptable response to her flirtation attempt. Instead, Elijah answered her honestly, leaving her baffled.

I had to press my lips together tightly to fight back the bubble of surprised laughter that threatened to escape me. As I did so, Elijah caught my eye and noticed my amusement. The corners of his lips turned up in a secret smile that we shared for a few moments before turning our attention back to the table.

Ever since then, Elijah and I had grown to understand each other on a deeper, intellectual level. It was hardly romantic. Rather, I simply knew that I could tell him anything, even the wildest thoughts inside my head, and he would do his very best to comprehend exactly what I meant.

I supposed we were friends. We clicked. We had many things in common—our introversion, our love of reading, our taste for peaceful solitude… what were the chances that a marriage my father arranged out of pure desperation turned out to be such a perfect match?

After our first dance, the rest of the ballroom filled with couples. I noticed my youngest sisters Danai and Sasha, dancing with their princes. Amalia, the fourth daughter of Zoren, was nowhere to be seen despite her fiancé Prince Declan of Savagery boisterously commanding a small portion of the crowd's attention, but she was even more antisocial than me, so I didn't think much of it.

Elijah and I parted ways inevitably. He had congratulations to accept from his parents and their closest advisors, and I had been beckoned across the room by Prince Finn, a gesture that I couldn't ignore.

The future King of Hell did not have his future queen, my sister, by his side. He greeted me alone, his cold and impassive features so flawless that they somewhat disturbed me. His vanity was palpable. Nothing and nobody should look as perfect as Finn did; the most beautiful things in nature are often the most poisonous. I supposed that was why Riven liked him, though.

He offered me a shallow bow, which I answered in kind with a deep curtsy.

"It seems I've misplaced my wife, but I'd like to extend our heartfelt congratulations to you and my brother," said Prince Finn, his tone as arrogant as the kingdom he ruled. "The two of you make a noticeably decent pair."

"Thank you," I replied. It was barely a compliment, but I knew what my role was in the conversation.

"Your heirs will be the most intellectual gods in the Underworld," Finn continued. "And perhaps the quietest."

I nodded, trying not to display the spark of annoyance I felt at the mention of heirs, as well as the subtly snide remark about mine and Elijah's shyness.

"Yes, perhaps," was all I said.

Clearly unable to get under my skin, Finn furrowed his brow slightly. He was used to being the most powerful prince, the most dominant man in the room—at least when his father wasn't present. The fact that I was making it too easy for him to assert himself above me confused him, especially because I was doing it with bored detachment.

Prince Finn didn't know that I cared little for status or shows of strength. True mightiness was in the mind; wit and cunning would get you much further than practiced sarcasm and blatant cruelty.

"Excuse me," Finn said after a moment. "Enjoy your evening, Princess Chloe."

I curtsied again and watched him go.

Elijah was on the other side of the ballroom speaking with one of his advisors and Prince Nico. I could've joined them, but I was desperately in need of some air.

Knowing that it wasn't exactly appropriate for me to sneak away from my own wedding reception, I glanced over my shoulder to check that, as I suspected, nobody was paying attention to me and slipped out of the ballroom. All I wanted was to leave the God of the Underworld's palace, go home to the humble palace in Disgrace, curl up with a good book, maybe admire my new wedding ring for a few minutes, and then go to sleep.

Until then, I would bide my time by skirting around the party in the wide, empty halls that snaked outwards from the ballroom. All of the palace staff were concentrated inside the reception serving drinks and hors d'oeuvres, so I didn't run into a single soul as I followed the moonlight toward the eastern balconies of the palace.

However, when I rounded the corner, I realized I wasn't the only person who decided to escape the event for a while.

Riven was alone on the nearest stone balcony.

I paused in the archway, halfway within and without, and frowned at her shadowed silhouette from the side. It wasn't like her to avoid crowds. She adored being the center of attention. Growing up, everything Riven did was an attempt to overcome her older twin's natural charm and win over the favor of everyone who crossed her path.

So then, what was she doing out here by herself?

She hadn't noticed me yet.

I squinted through the silvery illumination of the full moon and tried to get a closer look at her face. Riven appeared frozen in shock, her eyes wide and staring at the branch of a tree hanging over the railing of the balcony. There was nothing on the branch except for dense, velvety leaves. However, she was gazing at it as if something fearsome was resting amongst the foliage. That was also very odd. Riven wasn't afraid of anything.

Then I realized that I recognized her expression. It was the same one she wore, albeit briefly, on the day of Rose's trial. Back then, I watched her grow tense and horrified, eyes downcast, as if something demonic had slithered out of the shadows and embedded itself in the hems of her skirts… though nothing looked out of place to my eyes.

What in the Underworld could have my menacing sister so spooked?

Two tendencies warred within me—the natural curiosity that made me such an avid reader and the desire to not have anything to do with *the evil twin,* as my mother used to call her.

The former won out. With a sharp inhale, I emerged from the shadows and approached Riven. I stood on the opposite side of her and the apparently frightening tree branch and rested my palms gently on the cool stone of the railing. She didn't jump, nor did she do anything else to indicate that she was surprised by my sudden presence. Instead, Riven continued staring at the tree as if it was the only thing in the world.

I remained quiet, observing the darkness to see if I could figure out what had caused her to freeze up.

There was nothing. The tree was a grand, towering oak with lush leaves that rustled lightly in the nighttime breeze. There were no birds nor squirrels, nor beetles crawling across its smooth bark. It simply stood in the east gardens of the God of the Underworld's palace, unbothered and somewhat overgrown but otherwise harmless.

Finally, Riven spoke.

"Can you see it, too?" she whispered. Her voice was ragged with delicate panic, yet she still did not pull her eyes from the tree branch.

Her use of the word *it* sounded like she was referring to something much more ominous than a few leaves and twigs. I leaned forward to get a better look at her face, but Riven's unblinking eyes didn't meet mine.

"See what?" I asked.

Riven swallowed hard, her slender throat bobbing with the movement. She was dressed in pure gold silk, upstaging me and my wedding gown by miles.

"Can you hear it?" she murmured, ignoring my question.

I lifted a hand, reaching toward her timidly. I

hesitated to make contact. None of Zoren's daughters were particularly affectionate with each other. We were raised to see each other as competition, brought up to earn our father's godly favor above all else. Despite that, Rose had always been kind, and the youngest girls were known to be quite close, but Riven was never considered the ideal sister to seek friendship with.

"I think it followed me here," Riven said, her voice trembling. "I didn't think it would."

I checked the branch again.

Still nothing.

In our world of gods and goddesses, all manner of strange and mystical things could exist, but ghosts weren't among them. Immortals didn't die, half-mortals always passed on to the next life without delay, and mortal souls either found peace or were trapped forever in the prisons controlled by the God of the Underworld and his six sons. The idea of an unseen specter lurking in the King of Hell's castle was so preposterous that I waved it away instantly.

It occurred to me that Riven might be experiencing a psychotic break. Twenty-one years of debauchery had caught up to her, and her mind was finally crumbling.

Rather than suggest she was going insane, I

decided to play it cool. I didn't want to anger Riven and become a victim of her unforgiving wrath, let alone risk Elijah's relationship with Prince Finn, so I figured the casual route was the best one to take.

I let out a forced chuckle. "How much have you had to drink?"

That snapped her out of it.

She shook her head quickly and blinked her eyes, stepping away from the balcony and fixing me with a steady glare. The distress that painted her features into a pale, unfamiliar mask melted quickly into her trademark smirk. In an instant, Riven returned to the haughty, snobbish, mean-spirited girl I always knew her as.

She laughed. "How funny! I fooled the clever sister. I've been thinking about dabbling in the art of theatre, Chloe. I'm glad to know that my acting is very convincing. You look very concerned right now."

Anyone else would've believed her. Riven was an incredibly skilled actress, but she didn't need a stage to perform her craft. She fooled everyone with every calculating word that dripped from her tongue.

It wasn't worth it to challenge her. I merely pressed my hand to my chest and forced a shocked breath of laughter.

"How impressive," I exclaimed. "You really had me worried."

Riven sneered. "Yes, well, I should return to the party. My husband must be looking for me. Isn't yours? Oh—but, of course, he has probably run away to his own hiding place. What luck that he wasn't the firstborn. Otherwise, neither of you would be able to avoid the spotlight so easily."

She said everything as if it were a kindhearted observation, an inside joke we shared. Her poorly disguised insults slid right off me. I could see right through them.

"Yes, what luck," was all I said in response.

Riven flounced off without another word. When she was gone, I turned around to face the oak tree once more. I leaned as far over the railing as I dared without risking an accidental tumble over the edge and grabbed the branch Riven had been staring at. It was thin and flexible. I lifted it a few inches, observing the other branches around it and even pushing past the thick leaves to see if there was anything hidden in between them.

There was nothing.

I knew something of trees, oaks in particular. The one in front of me had a trunk that was about five feet in diameter, and it was so tall that it managed to drape over a fourth-floor balcony. Because of their ability to grow very large and to live for very long, oak trees were considered sacred by most gods. They were a good omen, a symbol of strength.

And yet, even oak trees had their limits. They could be cut down and turned into furniture for my father's study, a harp for the musically inclined Rose, or a dozen barrels for divine whiskey. Every autumn, their leaves turned brown and withered away. They stood bare against the cold, dull, and gray until spring returned and gave it permission to bloom again.

I preferred evergreens. So did my mother. Before she was seduced by Zoren and brought to live among the gods with a demigoddess growing in her womb, she was an arborist. In the mortal realm, her job had been to care for the trees in a vast botanical garden in a famous city located on a foggy bay.

My mother named me Chloe, but only because my father insisted. She wanted to name me after her favorite tree, the evergreen juniper. According to her, juniper berries are bitter and sometimes downright poisonous, so they were used in ancient religions favored by mortals to ward off evil spirits. I wasn't sure I would have lived up to the name, given that I was now a princess of Hell surrounded by the evil souls of twisted mortals, but I appreciated her wishful thinking.

You'd think that, given her affinity for trees, my mother would get along well with Zoren's wife, my stepmother. Gia was the goddess of evergreens, but she couldn't have cared less about the meaning behind my mother's failed choice for a name for me.

Gia hated all of us, mothers and daughters, without exception. She was a barren goddess and, admittedly, married to a romantic fool. Zoren's demigod children were a mocking slap to the face, a reminder that he sought out mortal women as mistresses over her because she couldn't give him the family he desired.

Although Gia despised me, I could only pity her.

At least she wasn't at the wedding. She wouldn't have been able to stomach the sight of her step-daughters entering into such advantageous marriages. She was a minor goddess, but jealousy was a powerful force. I imagined she would've been able to throw a Hell-worthy fit if she had to watch me walk down the aisle toward the third-eldest prince of the Underworld, who had a kingdom of his own that he would never be foolish enough to lose to the goddess of deceit, as my father had lost his.

I gazed up at the moon. It was working its way high into the sky. In a few hours, it would descend onto the western horizon and be replaced by the sun. Even in the realm of the gods, the galaxy spun its dependable rotations. I took comfort in that fact, knowing that even the most formidable beings in existence couldn't defeat the influences of the vast universe that expanded endlessly beyond us all.

I wondered what time it was. No one would expect Elijah and me to stay at the party all night. In their eyes, we had a marriage bed to get to. In reality, we would lie a respectful distance away from each other and read our respective novels until we silently fell asleep. We couldn't have an heir until I was made immortal. Otherwise, the little prince or princess wouldn't be a true god.

Not that I was eager to do… *that*. I'd perform my duties as expected, but children—and the act of making a child—was not currently on my list of priorities. Nor Elijah's, for that matter.

I bet that didn't stop Finn and Riven, though. There was probably some kind of divine magic trick they used to prevent Riven from getting pregnant with a demigod in the meantime. No one had dared to ask the God of the Underworld when we could expect to receive the gift of immortality, not even

Zoren himself, who brokered the deal in the first place. Assumably, the God of the Underworld would want to wait until all the marriages were sealed. Given that Prince Nico was single, and the youngest pair were still seventeen, it was logical to conclude that immortality would not come for a while.

That didn't bother me. Elijah didn't age as I did, but it wasn't as if I ran the risk of turning into an old crone while he enjoyed eternal youth. The six sons of the Underworld were born as grown men from the Red River, but their ages and birth order were taken very seriously. Though they could change their appearance at will, they each chose to appear as their natural selves—handsome young men with godly auras. Once I was made immortal, I could also appear pretty and youthful for eternity.

Footsteps echoed in the hallway beyond the balcony, nudging me out of my thoughts. I glanced over my shoulder to find Elijah approaching, smiling softly as he joined me at the railing. Wordlessly, he closed his eyes and tilted his face toward the sky, breathing in the fragrant air.

"I knew I would find you lost in thought on a balcony somewhere," he murmured, eyes still closed as the moon cast his face in an ethereal glow. "Unfortunately, it seems my father has an absurd number of balconies in his palace. This is the twenty-ninth one I've checked."

I grinned. "That's not so bad. The palace of the God of the Underworld has one hundred and fifty-seven balconies, so your journey to find me could have been much longer."

"You know so much. Practically everything," Elijah mused, opening his eyes and fixing me with an innocent, boyish smile. It was an endearing expression, one that made my heart thump erratically for the smallest of seconds. How could I not react that way when I was looking at the most striking man I'd ever seen?

"Not everything," I corrected him.

Elijah shook his head in disagreement. "I don't believe you. Tell me something you don't know."

It was a playful dare. Elijah and I were both fountains of knowledge. If there was something we didn't know, we could discuss it together and eventually reach a logical conclusion with our combined intellect.

I thought about telling Elijah that I didn't know why Riven just lied to me about her hallucination in the oak tree. I didn't know what she was seeing or hearing, nor did I know if it was real or if the Princess of Arrogance was losing her mind. It seemed like too much to elaborate on at the moment, so instead, I took a chance and smirked at Elijah.

"I do not know your father's true name," I murmured.

Anyone else would've gasped and taken a step back, shocked that I had the gall to even mention such a thing. Knowing the God of the Underworld's true name was an impossible feat, a secret guarded with a bloody curse. To know his name and to utter it aloud was blasphemous, a one-way ticket to eternal damnation and unending pain. That was because the God of the Underworld's real name was the key to Hell. If you wielded it, you could claim the Underworld as your own.

Elijah wasn't scandalized by my statement. Instead, he burst out laughing.

"Fair enough," he chuckled. "We can suffer the lack of that specific knowledge together."

"Isn't that what marriage is all about?" I joked.

"I believe it is," he nodded with faux solemnity.

I bit my lip nervously, looking at the archway that would lead us back inside to the reception.

"Do you think it's over yet?" I asked. "Do you think we can leave?"

"I hope so," he sighed. "Everyone in there knows

we aren't party animals. Plus, it's nearly midnight. Perhaps if we keel over with exhaustion in the middle of the ballroom, my father will dismiss us, and we can return to Disgrace."

Returning to Disgrace sounded like a godsend. It was a small, humble palace located several hours' journey from the God of the Underworld's central city. Surrounded by misty forests and babbling brooks, the isolated kingdom was exactly the place I could picture myself living for eternity. It was peaceful and quiet, and we hardly ever received visitors. Better yet, when Elijah learned that his wife-to-be enjoyed reading, the library was expanded by thousands of volumes, and the number of crackling fireplaces and cozy nooks increased as well. It was a dream. Some nights, I even fell asleep in the library of Disgrace, soothed by the pattering of rain on the windows and the gorgeous words floating through my mind like a melody.

"Must we keel over?" I laughed. "Can't we simply ask nicely?"

"Why didn't I think of that?" Elijah replied with a grin. "You truly are the brains of this operation."

Something had shifted between us since we said our vows. Before, we were friendly with each other, but it was nothing like the warm glances and playful quips we were tossing back and forth now. The reality of our eternal promise to each other was inescapable; it seemed as though we made a silent agreement not to fight it. Even if I did not fall in love with Elijah, at least I would have a friend to share my immortality with. Wasn't that the best anyone in an arranged marriage could hope for?

Elijah held out his arm for me, and I tucked my hand into the crook of his elbow, following him off the balcony and away from the mysterious branch of the oak tree. By the time we made it back to the ballroom, the party had spilled out across other parts of the palace, gods and royals and nobles dripping down the staircases and across candlelit parlors. Grateful to be free of the expectation to dance in the grand ballroom, Elijah and I followed the stream of people down to the main entrance hall of the God of the Underworld's palace in hopes of tracking him down and asking for permission to leave.

Freedom was within my grasp. Once I left, I never had to come back… unless another one of my sisters decided to run away, and I was forced out of bed and dumped before the furious god's throne again. I'd never have to see Riven again, nor be reminded of her anguishing twin, trapped in the darkest pits of Hell for the next fifty years because she fell in love with the wrong man. No more trials or public executions, at least not for a while. When Amalia and Prince Declan were married, or if Nico found a new match and beat them to the punch, I would have to return, but I wouldn't be the object of attention in those circumstances. Elijah and I could pay our respects and duck out early.

When we finally caught sight of the God of the Underworld, Elijah sighed under his breath. Confused, I glanced up at my new husband, but he was frowning at his father with an unreadable expression.

As the hall filled up with the majority of the party guests, the God of the Underworld planted his feet before the exit and crossed his arms, smiling at his son and me as if he'd been expecting us to meet him there at this exact time.

And as if the night was far from over.

CHAPTER 3

"Gather around, please," the God of the Underworld proclaimed, his voice echoing loudly enough to be heard over the cacophony of a thousand other voices. "If my sons and the daughters of Zoren could come forward, I have an announcement I'd like to make."

"For once, I wish my father retire for the evening without making a grand declaration," Elijah muttered. I squeezed his arm encouragingly as we stepped in front of the crowd that formed a respectful arc around the god.

I spotted the others, including Finn and Riven. Nico, Amalia, and Declan were several yards away, waiting at the front of the throng, too. My two youngest sisters and their fiancés hovered closest to the God of the Underworld, with our father Zoren standing right behind them. Raya was nowhere to be seen, likely having returned to the Red River. Everyone knew she hated emerging from its scarlet depths, but the weddings of her sons could hardly be skipped.

"I have made a decision," said the God of the Underworld. "We have all enjoyed two very beautiful weddings these past few weeks, and I have appreciated having my sons back home in my palace. My decision is not permanent, but it will remain as law for at least the next year."

My stomach turned, filling with dread. I had a feeling I already knew what he was about to say. However, one look at Finn and Riven told me that even they weren't privy to whatever decision the God of the Underworld made in the past hour or so.

"Given recent events," the God of the Underworld continued. "I have decided that my children and their wives or fiancées will live in my palace rather than their respective kingdoms. This includes Prince Nico."

It took everything within me not to deflate with disappointment. Elijah clearly felt the same way, placing his other hand over the one I was clutching his arm with and squeezing it gently.

"We have suffered many complications due to the poor choices of the demigoddess Rose. As such, I would like to keep an eye on everyone and ensure that all matches are progressing positively," said the God of the Underworld, narrowing his eyes as a few murmurs rose from the crowd, which quieted them instantly. "But don't worry! Prince Elijah and Princess Chloe will enjoy a beautiful, private wedding suite in the east wing, and I encourage them to indulge in this privilege despite the new arrangement. Similarly, the newly married Prince Finn and Princess Riven will also be in the large family suite in the south wing. All other princes and demigoddess will find that their appropriately *separate* bedrooms have already been arranged for them in the north wing."

A few playful titters began at the emphasis, implying the raging young hormones that many believed ruled our minds. From the looks on my sisters' faces, however, they were not bothered by the forced separation. Like me, they all appeared baffled by the prospect that none of us would be going home that night.

I wanted to cry. I wanted to throw a temper tantrum. I wanted to shove past the God of the Underworld and run back to the tranquility of

Disgrace. I didn't want to live with my sisters again. Learning that I would be freed from my father's household and finally given a chance to separate myself from the pressures of sibling rivalry was welcome news. I didn't want to go back to the way life was before. As unexpected as it was, I'd been relatively happy with my new life in the Underworld.

And now I was going to have to play house with my sisters and their boyfriends because the God of the Underworld didn't trust that any of us could handle courtship without living under his watchful gaze.

At least Riven looked upset, too. She'd already accomplished so much for herself. The throne of Arrogance was a trophy she won with pure sharp-witted deceit. She didn't want to give it up, even temporarily. Prince Finn also looked like he wanted to fight his father's edict. His arrogant personality made it impossible for him to digest the regressive act of moving back in with his parent.

It didn't matter how any of us felt about it. The King of Hell's word was law.

"Any questions?" he asked the crowd. When met with silence, he clapped his hands together and smiled widely. "Wonderful! In that case, join me in sending off the newlyweds, not to the kingdom of Disgrace, but to their new home in the east wing!"

All eyes were on Elijah and me. We couldn't scowl or pout. We couldn't escape. As the dense herd of wedding guests parted like the sea to allow us to carry on our way, all we could do was smile and wave at the applauding mass. High above our heads, where the ceiling of the grand hall opened up to the sky, fireworks popped and sizzled in an array of colors. They flashed against the marble, a kaleidoscope of dizzying bursts that made my head spin as I tried to process the path ahead.

When we passed out of the roofless hall, the fireworks didn't stop. The entire walk to the east wing was lit by hundreds of tiny pops of light on the ceiling and raining down with harmless sparks. It was an embarrassingly dramatic display of celebration, something concocted by the God of the Underworld as a gift for us but far too flashy for our tastes.

Everyone clapped and cheered as we marched through the sprawling palace. Elbows were thrown out by those attempting to jostle through the crowd and catch a glimpse of us, heads poking up hungrily from behind taller shoulders. It was ridiculous. They already knew what we looked like. Mere weeks ago, they got a clear view of both Elijah and me when we sat in the stands to watch that servant boy hang and my sister punished. On top of that, they had all day and night to drink in the sight of us during the wedding ceremony and reception. Why were they suddenly acting like we were elusive celebrities?

I felt like an animal at the zoo.

The entrance to our suite was as obvious as it was embarrassing. An archway of ivy and wisteria had been constructed over the double doors, and a carpet of tiny petals fluttered under our feet. Elijah didn't hesitate to march right through it and throw open the door, tugging me inside with him.

When the door shut again and the latch clicked into place, the racket from outside all but disappeared. Together, we collected ourselves and observed the luxurious suite that we'd been sentenced to call home for the next year. As expected, everything was done in dark materials and fabrics, from the black oak furniture to the emerald velvet bedding. The large reception parlor we entered led to a smaller, more intimate sitting area complete with a roaring fire and plush seating. On the left, a mahogany door opened to a comfortable study for Elijah to conduct his princely affairs in. On the other side of the room, a more feminine office had been arranged for me to work in.

Beyond was the bedroom. Neither one of us said a word as we stepped into the colossal chamber that was three times bigger than the room we planned to share at the palace of Disgrace. A bed the size of a boat and as fluffy as a cloud sat under a domed ceiling painted with flowering vines and vibrant birds. Massive wardrobes stood at the other end of the bedroom, both of them stuffed full of clothes for us to use in our temporary residence. The bathroom was just as grand, featuring a clawfoot tub big enough for at least four people and a vanity that was too large to suit my humble beauty preferences.

"This is where the visiting gods and goddesses used to stay when I was a kid," Elijah mused. "Like, the really important ones."

"He certainly went to a lot of trouble for us," I replied, glancing out the French doors to see that we had a large balcony of our own attached to the bedroom.

"I don't understand why we have to be here," he grumbled, sinking down onto the chaise at the foot of the bed. "Finn and Riven, too. If he wants to keep an eye on the others, that makes sense, but we're already married."

I shrugged. "Maybe he's just trying to make it seem fair. At least the party is over now."

Elijah snorted and then ran his fingers through his dark, auburn-streaked hair.

"I'm sorry." He sighed.

I sat down next to him. I was itching to get out of my wedding dress, but it felt too awkward to slip into the bathroom for some privacy at that moment. We were friendly, but we'd never slept in the same room before, which also meant that things like getting dressed—or rather, undressed—for bed also hadn't come up yet.

"What for?" I asked.

"This really isn't how I intended for our wedding night to go," he admitted, clasping his hands together in his lap.

I raised my eyebrows at him. "Oh? And how did you intend for it to go?"

A light blush crept onto his cheeks as the hidden meaning behind my question sat screaming between us. Suddenly, it felt like the bed was even bigger.

Elijah groaned and dropped his head into his hands, leaning forward to rest his elbows on his knees.

"That's not what I meant," he replied, voice muffled by his hands.

I laughed at his bashfulness, though I was also blushing. Timidly, I reached out and patted his back.

"It's okay," I told him. "I know you didn't mean… *that*. I know we're not really at that point in our, um, relationship yet."

"Arranged marriages are weird."

"Agreed."

Suddenly, Elijah sat up and looked at me with an anxious expression.

"I mean, not that I think it's weird to be married to you," he corrected himself. "It's just odd to think that we're bound together for eternity, but the highest level of intimacy we've shared is holding hands—well, I guess I kissed you on the cheek at the ceremony… don't get me wrong, though. It's not that I'm unhappy to be married to you. Not at all. You're beautiful. You're smart and witty, and you're the first person who ever really understood my sarcasm. I'm — I-I am very fond of you. And I'm really very content to take things slow with you. I hope you don't think that I expect—"

"Elijah, for the love of the gods, breathe," I chuckled, placing my hand over his and fixing him with an earnest gaze. On the surface, I hoped I looked like a calm, patient wife. Inside, I was on fire. He thought I was beautiful. He thought I was smart. He felt the connection between us just like I did.

Of course, I'd always known that Elijah at least

didn't hate me, but he'd never said anything like *that* out loud before.

"Sorry," he replied with a slow exhale. "I'm jittery. We have such comfortable lives in Disgrace. Knowing that we're going to be stuck here for a while makes me feel a bit anxious."

"You're not very close with your brothers, are you?"

It was an obvious fact, but I asked the question anyway.

Elijah shook his head. "Not really. Finn's cold as ice, Nico parties too much, and Declan is downright unpleasant to be in the same room with. Sebastian and Caleb are decent, but they're also very young."

"I'm not close with my sisters either."

"I figured. The fact that Riven stole her twin's fiancé the second she got the chance told me everything I needed to know about the sibling dynamics in Zoren's kingdom."

A bubble of laughter escaped me. He said it so candidly. Nobody else had dared to gossip about Riven's smooth transition from the second-born prince to the first, even though it was a bit scandalous. That was probably because most people preferred to have Riven by Finn's side. For all her beauty and grace, Rose wasn't the formidable future queen the Underworld had hoped for. I wouldn't be surprised if those who saw right through her scheming were impressed by her ferocious ambition.

"Well," I said, nervously glancing down at my feet. "At least we have each other. I truly do enjoy your company."

"Really?" Elijah grinned. "I mean… likewise."

I held out my palm for a handshake. "Friends?"

Without hesitation, Elijah grabbed my hand and shook it. "Friends."

"Good," I sighed. "I don't think I've ever really had a friend before."

"Me either," Elijah admitted. "Also, don't take this the wrong way, but as your friend, would you like me to help you untie that corset? It looks really uncomfortable."

The blush returned to my cheeks, but I sighed in relief at the offer. My

"Yes, please," I replied, standing up and kicking off the high, pointed heels I'd been wearing since noon. I sank down several inches, sighing happily as the punished balls of my feet touched the cool marble underfoot.

"I thought you looked taller than usual," Elijah quipped, rising from the chaise and coming to stand behind me.

"There's a layer of pearl buttons," I instructed him. "And then underneath are the corset strings. You can just loosen them, and then I'll be able to get it off myself."

"Right."

He cleared his throat. Several seconds of nervous hesitation followed, and then I felt his fingers carefully undoing the buttons at the back of my satin gown. Earlier that day, a crew of royal maids dressed me, tying and buttoning me up with expert precision. The personal maid I'd grown used to in Disgrace, a girl named Milou, was probably pacing back and forth in my old bedchamber, wondering when I'd be back. Hopefully, she wouldn't be too bored in my prolonged absence.

Both of us fell into silence while Elijah worked. He finished with the buttons and lightly pushed the loosened fabric aside. I clasped my arms in front of myself to keep the dress from falling.

"They knotted this really tightly," Elijah murmured, fiddling with the strings at the base of the corset just above my tailbone. "We should outlaw these when we get back to Disgrace."

I giggled. "You're a truly inspiring politician."

"I try my best."

Finally, he got the knot undone and started

pulling the corset apart. With each tug of his fingers, it became easier to breathe. I relaxed more with every passing second, grateful for the gentle touch of his hands. When he was done, I stepped away, clutching my clothes to myself, and bustled into the bathroom with a whispered, "Thank you."

Once I was in privacy, I let the dress, the corset, and all the complicated undergarments fall to the floor. There was a nightgown hanging nearby, a frilly thing made of gossamer that was definitely meant for a couple that would be sharing their marriage bed the traditional way—if that's what you wanted to call it—but it was my only option. Thankfully, there was also a silk robe with a long hem that covered the rest of me. I bundled myself up inside it and then hurried over to the vanity, where I plucked out the seemingly thousands of pearl pins in my hair and then used my fingers to comb out the crown of braids I'd been wearing.

What I was left with was a head of wild, shoulder-length curls. The voluminous twists were a feature I got from my mother, as well as her golden-brown skin. I stared at my reflection in the mirror. Without the dress and the elaborate hairstyle, I looked much younger. I always had a youthful faith, but suddenly I wondered if my soft, freckled cheeks made me look too childish.

"My baby-faced girl and her big brain," my mother used to say with a sigh, lightly poking my dimples or ruffling my hair. Even when I turned eighteen, nobody ever referred to me as pretty or dignified. All I ever got was *cute* and *adorable*.

But Elijah thought I was beautiful.

And he was also waiting for me to stop taking so long in the bathroom.

Crossing my arms against my chest, I entered the bedroom once more and found that Elijah had pulled down the covers of the bed. He was propped up on the pillows on one side, leaving several feet of space for me to sleep comfortably on the other. I hopped up onto the mattress and settled down in the soft sheets. At least the bed in my gilded prison was comfortable.

And at least the boy I had to share it with wasn't arrogant like Finn or spiteful like Nico. All things considered, I felt lucky.

While I'd fought with my hairpins, Elijah had changed into simple cotton pajamas. He looked different when he wasn't stiffly tucked into a royal ensemble. I liked him better like this.

"I looked for something to read, but there isn't a

single book in this entire suite," Elijah reported. "Maybe we can arrange to have some things shipped in from Disgrace."

I nodded, pulling the covers up to my chin. I was tired enough from the day's events that, for once, I didn't need to lull myself into sleep with a novel. My eyes were falling shut easily on their own.

"Hey, Chloe," Elijah whispered, blowing out the candle on his bedside table and laying down on his respective half of the mattress.

But I was already half asleep at that point, drifting into unconsciousness with such swiftness that there was no way I could find the strength to pull myself out of it to answer him. Despite the fact that I'd never shared a bed with a boy before, let alone in the home of one of the most powerful gods in existence, I felt completely at ease.

Whatever he wanted to tell me, it would have to wait until morning.

My dreams that night were dark and tense, the antithesis to the peaceful warmth I felt when I drifted to sleep.

At first, the dream started out as a memory. I was nine years old but small for my age that I was often mistaken for being much younger. It was a pleasant summer day, and I was curled up in the branches of a tree in my father's apple orchard with a novel. The dream was so detailed that I could recall the name of the book. *Great Expectations* by Charles Dickens. My father loved literature from the mortal realm, and so did I. There was something so fascinating about reading books written by mortals. Their imaginations were vivid and magical, even though they themselves were so dull and ordinary.

True to the memory, there was a rustling in the branches above me. A pale face and long, tangled hair stared at me through the leaves.

Riven.

Although only ten years old, Riven was as graceful and strong as any adult demigod. Her physical abilities were so impressive and her personality so alluring that many mistook her for our father's firstborn.

I knew she liked to climb the trees around the palace, but I didn't think I would run into her in the relatively short apple trees.

Riven dropped down onto the thick branch beside mine, though the tree barely even trembled from her movement. She stared at me coolly, then grabbed a ripe apple that hung over her head and bit into it fiercely, the juice running down her chin.

"Why do you read so much?" she asked me, wiping her face with the back of her hand. "You know none of those stories are real, right?"

"Yes," I responded. "That is precisely why I enjoy them."

"You're weird," Riven remarked. "Your mom is weird, too."

It wasn't the first insult she'd thrown at my mother and me, so it didn't bother me. While the rest of us, even six-year-old Sasha, chose to ignore each other, Riven barreled down the path of offense, treating each of her sisters like a difficult obstacle to overcome rather than a fellow being.

"We are all a little weird, and life's a little weird," I replied, eyes focused on the page in front of me though I wasn't absorbing any of the words.

"What?"

"It's Dr. Seuss."

"Who?"

"An author. Mortal."

"Is he dead?" asked Riven.

"I think so."

"Do you think he's in the Underworld? You know what the Underworld is, right?"

"Of course I do," I sighed. "And no, I'm sure his soul passed on to a peaceful place. His books are nice. They have good messages."

"Whatever," Riven snapped, tossing her half-finished apple onto the ground and stretching up to hang from one of the taller branches.

She was quiet for a moment, so I dared to hope she would get bored and leave me alone soon. Unfortunately, I was wrong.

Riven crouched down on the limb beside mine again, a devious smirk on her face.

"Did you know that mortals sometimes kill each other by hanging people from trees?" she asked.

I feigned indifference, turning the page of my book though I hadn't finished what was on the previous one.

"Yes, I did know that," I answered.

"How?" she challenged.

"I read it in a book."

"Gods, you're so annoying," grumbled Riven. Then, with a mischievous snicker, she reached out and shoved me out of the tree.

The fall wasn't far, maybe eight or nine feet, but I wasn't prepared for it. I landed hard on my side, my forehead cracking against an exposed root and a sharp *snap* indicating that my wrist was broken. My book landed beside me a second later, unharmed.

I groaned and sat up, pressing my uninjured hand to my head. My palm came away bloody. I glared up at Riven, who was smirking at me from high above.

"Oops," she giggled. "Maybe you shouldn't be so clumsy, bookworm."

A pair of footsteps in the grass caused both of us to glance behind me before I could articulate a response to my cruel older sister.

Danai, the fifth daughter, and her willowy

mother stood frozen in the orchard, a few trees away. From the looks on their faces, they saw everything. However, I already knew that the older woman wasn't going to help me. As Danai began to whimper at the sight of my blood, her mother took her hand and steered her away, hurrying both of them out of the orchard without a backward glance.

Riven landed on her feet in the grass beside me a second later. She offered me her hand, but I ignored it. I knew better. She'd probably pull me up halfway and then shoved me back down again. That was her idea of a fun prank. Instead of accepting her help, I struggled to my feet and grabbed my book, turning to go inside where my mother could tend to my throbbing wrist.

However, by the time I was on my feet, the ground had changed from lush green grass to cold gray stone. It was no longer a summer afternoon but an early autumn evening. The moon was full and bright.

Somehow, though I'd been a nine-year-old a moment before, I knew that I was now twenty and in the Underworld. I was on the same balcony where I found Riven by herself on my wedding night, though this memory was somewhat distorted.

Riven wasn't standing at the railing but perched

on the thick branch that stretched over it. The leaves attempted to obscure her, but her doll-like beauty was impossible to hide.

As usual, she was smirking at me.

"Shouldn't you be dancing with your new husband or something?" she asked me.

In the dream, I was better at talking back to her.

"I could ask you the same thing," I quipped.

Riven rolled her eyes. "Don't be rude, Chloe. Everyone knows that Prince Finn is dead now."

"Wait, what?"

"Yeah, don't you remember? The God of the Underworld said that if I could beat him in a duel, I could take his place and be the sole ruler of Arrogance and the future Queen of Hell all by myself," Riven chuckled as if she was explaining an obvious concept to a confused child.

"That doesn't make sense," I argued. "Prince Finn is a god. He can't die."

Riven shifted on the branch, her gold gown falling gracefully around her as if the oak itself was bleeding finery.

"They only tell us that because they don't want us to know that the opposite is actually true," the dream-version of Riven corrected me sternly. "I would think that someone as smart as you would've figured that out by now. Anyway, do you want to know how I killed him?"

"Shouldn't I already know that, too?" I asked.

"Nope," Riven replied with a grin. "I haven't told anyone the truth about how I did it. All they know is that he's dead."

My subconscious was not as freaked out by the conversation as it should've been. I merely shrugged my shoulders at my demonic sister.

"How, then?" I inquired.

She leaned forward conspiratorially, the large tree seemingly mirroring her movements.

"A snake," she answered.

"A snake?"

"Mhm. A poisonous one. I set it free inside his bed. It took a lot of venom to put the young god down, but the snake wanted to help me. Do you want to help me too, Chloe?"

A strange rush of sound met my ears. It sounded like something was sliding against the stone beneath me, but I couldn't seem to take my eyes off Riven to figure out what it was.

"What do you want my help with?" I asked her.

"Well, if I tell you before you agree, I'll have to kill you."

The animalistic whisper, like metal against

marble, grew louder. Finally, I managed to maneuver my body around.

What I saw caused me to stumble backward.

It was a snake. Impossibly large, in terms of both width and length, it slithered across the balcony toward me. The creature was black as ink, though the shine of the moon revealed the slightest touch of iridescence in its scales.

The snake let out a hiss.

Riven cackled. "It's telling me that it already knows you're going to refuse me. It says that you're not on my side."

Since when could my sister talk to snakes?

"Riven, what—" I began, but the snake raised its head and revealed a pair of needle-sharp fangs which glinted silver.

"I guess I'll have to kill you, too," my sister sighed.

The leaves rustled behind me, but I didn't dare take my eyes off the snake.

It was too late anyway. Before I could take another step backward, the snake lunged fast as lightning and sank its teeth into my throat—

BY THE TIME MY EYES FLEW OPEN, THE DREAM WAS already forgotten, and yet I couldn't shake the eerie feeling that made my skin crawl with goosebumps when I sat up and took in my surroundings.

It took me a minute to remember why the room was so unfamiliar.

But then I remembered everything.

I was married now.

I lived in the God of the Underworld's palace now.

I shared a bed with Prince Elijah, who might be the first friend I've ever had, now.

It was a mixed bag of realizations.

The morning sunlight was pouring through the windows with golden ferocity. I blinked against the harsh light, cursing the fact that we forgot to close the curtains before going to sleep. Usually, my maid, Milou, took care of those things for me so I could at least rest a couple of hours past dawn.

It was cold, too. The fire in the hearth had died out in the middle of the night, leaving the room—which was made of not-so-cozy marble, of course—frigid as the autumn air crept inside.

I glanced over at Elijah, who was fast asleep despite the fact that a shard of sunlight was glowing against his face. He slept on his stomach, his head turned toward me, with one of his cheeks squashed into the pillow. His hair, just long enough to curl around his ears, was a tangled mess. Still, he looked like an angel with his features effortlessly smooth with sleep.

I couldn't help but smile.

I'd learned so many things about him in the past day alone. My husband thought I was beautiful. My husband got adorably nervous at the thought of undoing my corset strings. My husband was a heavy sleeper.

Carefully, I slipped out of bed and padded across the room. I grabbed a few things from the wardrobe —some undergarments and a loose gown made of a comfortable cotton material dyed emerald green.

In the bathroom, I rubbed the tiredness from my eyes and drew a bath. Washing up quickly in the blessedly warm water, I puzzled over why I woke up feeling so disturbed. It was as if I'd had a nightmare, but I couldn't remember a thing.

Maybe it was just the general sense of dread I felt at the prospect of sharing a home with my sisters again. Especially Riven. Having her close by was rarely a good thing.

I got ready quickly, dressing in the flowing gown I picked out with ease and foregoing a corset entirely. I combed my unruly curls back into two neat braids and then spent a moment fretting over the fine jewels the God of the Underworld had laid out for me in the drawers of the vanity table. Beautiful necklaces, earrings, and bracelets sparkled in the persistent sun, but I'd never been a big fan of jewelry.

There was one accessory that I couldn't go without... my wedding ring, set with a large emerald in a platinum gold band. Each of the prince's kingdoms had its own distinctive colors. If Riven had married Prince Nico, her ring would've been obsidian framed in silver, but marrying Prince Finn of Arrogance had instead given her a massive ruby encased in delicate gold.

I liked the ring I wore. It was pretty but not ostentatious.

I emerged from the bathroom at last, though one glance at the clock told me barely half an hour had passed.

Elijah was stretching languidly in bed when I entered the room. He blushed at the sight of me and quickly lowered his arms.

"Good morning," he said, his voice rough with sleep.

I offered him a timid smile. "Good morning."

"Do you normally wake up this early?"

"Not usually," I shrugged. "But I don't sleep very late either."

"A happy medium. Me, too."

Feeling nervous about the shared living space and the inexplicable tension between us that wasn't entirely unpleasant, I went back to the wardrobe and managed to locate a pair of leather brogues. They weren't traditional princess attire, but the God of the Underworld must've known that I preferred shoes that were flat and comfortable. Maybe he could sense the pain I was in yesterday.

I didn't realize Elijah was right behind me until he spoke again.

"I was thinking," he began, causing me to jump with surprise. He flushed, his eyes full of apology when he realized he got out of bed way too quietly. "We should make the best out of this situation. I mean, it's really our younger siblings who will be paid the most attention to, and we don't have as many responsibilities as Finn and Riven do, so we kind of have free access to my father's palace."

"So, what should we do?" I asked.

"Well, the library…"

I instantly perked up.

How could I have forgotten? The Library of the Underworld was an immortal treasure. It was home to nearly every tome, both fiction and nonfiction, known to mortals and immortals. It wasn't open to the public, but everyone knew that guests of the God of the Underworld were welcome to make use of it to their heart's content. That was part of the reason why so many immortal scholars were constantly attempting to get on the god's good side. An invitation to the Underworld was an academic dream come true.

And as nice as the library in Disgrace was, it was nothing compared to the one inside this palace. Maybe there was a silver lining to this situation after all.

"Yes," I said to Elijah excitedly, though he hadn't asked me a question. "Yes, please! Show me where it is!"

He chuckled, eyes sparkling with laughter at my reaction.

"Alright, alright," he replied. "I'll get dressed."

I tried to be patient as he disappeared into the bathroom, pacing through the various rooms of the suite. I looked again at my office, wondering how many books I could carry at once from the library and store in there. Would the God of the Underworld allow that? What harm could it do as long as I wasn't taking the books out of the palace?

Elijah didn't take long. He found me in the reception parlor, drumming my fingertips on the mantle of the fireplace. Apparently, he also decided to dress casually. If not for the absurdly opulent setting, I would think that we were about to embark on an average day in Disgrace, working on our own studious endeavors in measured silence and respectful solitude.

"Okay, come on," Elijah murmured eagerly, taking my hand and pulling me toward the door.

However, just as he was about to reach for the knob, it turned, and the door was opened by someone on the other side. Startled, both Elijah and I froze. Hadn't the God of the Underworld promised us privacy? Was someone trying to sneak into our suite when they thought we would still be asleep?

A teenage boy dressed in plain black clothes poked his head through the crack. He was a servant.

"Sorry, Your Highnesses!" he squeaked. "I just came to tend to the hearths. I apologize for disturbing you!"

"No worries," said Elijah patiently. "Come on in. We were just heading out. Thank you."

The young servant looked both surprised and

relieved by Elijah's kindness. He nodded quickly and shuffled into the room, scurrying over the fireplace with his head down.

Then, with a breathtaking smile that made me forget where in the world I was, Elijah led me out of the room and down the sunlit hall. Once full of wedding guests applauding for us, it was now blissfully empty.

CHAPTER 5

The Library of the Underworld was everything I hoped for but struggled to visualize. It was difficult to conceptualize how every single book in the world could fit into one room.

When I saw the explanation with my own eyes, I was struck speechless.

The library was, of course, very big. Numerous rows of shelves spread out from the center like a maze. From my vantage point in the carpeted entry hall strewn with old leather armchairs and mismatched tables, I couldn't see the end of it However, it wasn't until I looked up at the ceiling when I realized where most of the books *actually* were.

In fact, the library had no ceiling at all. Just like the grand hall where the God of the Underworld greeted his guests from an imperious throne, the library had been constructed with divine power. Instead of opening up to the sky, however, the ceiling of the library stretched into infinity, the shelves towering so high that they turned into nothing but tiny points in the distance.

I'd seen many displays of the King of Hell's power—furious hurricanes, magically transportive fog, and merciless punishment—but this was the first time I didn't see it as a frightening thing.

This was what all the gods should've been doing with their power. How could you want for anything else when every piece of knowledge ever written down was at your fingertips?

"—it's organized vaguely by genre," Elijah was explaining, though I struggled to make sense of his words as I continued to marvel at the wonders in front of me. "And by that, I mean *very* vaguely. As in, fiction is to the north and east, nonfiction to the south and west. Within those shelves, they're only categorized by the date the book was written. The most recent volumes will be on the bottom, and the ancient texts will be all the way up there."

"So, how do I…?" I trailed off, choosing instead to point vaguely at the ceiling-not-ceiling rather than finish my question aloud.

"Oh, right," he chuckled. "I left that detail out, didn't I? The library responds to intellectual desire. Basically, all you have to do is *want* to read something, and the library will deliver it. You can think of a specific title or a question you want answered, or a topic you're intrigued by, and the library will give you exactly what you need."

"That's insane."

"Tell me about," he agreed. "Just be careful, though. Try to be as specific as possible when thinking about what you need. When I was younger, I came in here looking for information about political ethics, and I was practically buried under a mountain of nearly every single philosopher who's ever lived."

"Got it."

"The most comfortable seats are along the south wall. There's a red sofa that I basically lived on before my father gave us our own kingdoms," Elijah continued. "I'd show you the way myself, but I actually have to go do something."

Before I could catch myself, I frowned with

disappointment. I'd been under the impression we would be exploring the library together. I was hoping for a chance to talk to him more, to nurture our friendship with the interest we shared. We spent so many months being shy and non-conversational; the shift that occurred last night between them felt nice.

But perhaps it was temporary, a symptom of the drama of our wedding day.

I hoped not.

"What is it?" I asked him. If I was his wife now, wasn't I allowed to ask him where he was going?

"It's just government stuff," he replied quickly, his gaze clouding over as if he wasn't telling the truth. "You know, matters of state. Boring things my father wants me to take care of… stuff like that…"

He was lying. Even an idiot would be able to tell.

However, I didn't bother questioning him further. I didn't want to pry and risk getting in an argument on our first official day of being married. Plus, it's not like he was under an obligation to tell me every single detail of his daily schedule. We rarely kept each other in the loop when we lived in Disgrace, so why would we start now?

Maybe he was telling the truth, and I was just feeling paranoid after the weird sensation I woke up with. Perhaps the reason he sounded so nervous was because he didn't want to make me feel bad about the fact that I was clearly not included in whatever political meetings were happening that day, despite being an official princess of the Underworld.

I forced an easy smile onto my face.

"Sure, no problem," I told him. "I'm sure I'll be in here all day."

"I'll come find you before dinner."

"Sounds good."

Parting ways was awkward. A goodbye hug felt stupid, a kiss on the cheek too intimate for a budding friendship. We ended up waving to each other as he ducked out of the library and disappeared around the corner.

Shaking off that odd turn of events, I faced the limitless shelves. The library was empty, much like the halls. It seemed that, after we went to sleep last night, the God of the Underworld was quick to clear the wedding guests out of his home. Everything was spotless, too. The servants likely worked through the night to put everything back in its place. They would have to go to the trouble four more times over the next year. I hoped they were compensated fairly.

I bit my lip and wandered into the nonfiction section, stepping within the narrow aisle between two shelves on the south side of the room. Even with the answer to everything ready to be delivered on a whim, I didn't struggle to find a topic to research. I hadn't stopped thinking about it for weeks, but life was so hectic with the two weddings that I couldn't spare a moment to dig deep. Thanks to the God of the Underworld's unexpected decision, I finally had the chance.

The only problem was that my research topic would probably be frowned upon by him. Hopefully, he didn't get a receipt of everything that was researched in his library.

"Okay," I whispered. In front of me was a shelf full of instruction manuals about how to operate strange mortal technology I'd never heard of.

I closed my eyes because that felt like the right thing to do.

Okay, magical library... please give me information about the darkest pits of Hell. What is it like down there?

Even though I wasn't close to Rose, I worried about her. The darkest pits of Hell was a prison reserved for immortals who couldn't be killed. She was just a demigoddess, half-mortal and gentle in nature. I would never vocally disagree with the God of the Underworld's choice of punishment, but I did secretly believe that it was too harsh. She was my sister, after all. It didn't matter if we didn't have the same mother. We were tied together by our father's divine blood. If the rest of my sisters didn't care what happened to Rose for the next fifty years, that was their choice.

I, on the other hand, sought to quell my anxiety with knowledge.

A soft *thump* caused me to open my eyes. At my feet, a black book with a plain linen cover had landed, assumably from high above. Despite the topic, I grinned with glee. It was working.

As I stooped to pick it up, another book landed on top of it, causing me to step back with a gasp. This one was thinner, with a cover the color of steeped tea. I looked up just in time to watch a leather-bound tome fall from a shelf at least a hundred feet high. It should've landed with a deafening *smack* on the tile, but the library slowed its descent at the last moment, and it dropped onto the stack with a polite puff of dust.

I waited for more to come, but the sky seemed to have stopped raining books.

"That's it?" I asked out loud.

In reply, a long wooden cylinder rolled down the aisle and bumped against the toes of my shoes. It was the kind of container that usually contained a map or a diagram.

I frowned when nothing else came. Three books and a tube of rolled-up parchment? Of all the books in the world, these were the only ones that mentioned the darkest pits of Hell?

The more I thought about it, the more I realized it made perfect sense. I was specific in my pursuit, asking the library to tell me what the darkest pits of Hell were like, not the history of them or who was down there. Furthermore, it was a safe bet the library also knew only to give me volumes in a language that I could read. I'd learned a handful of languages, most of them mortal, for the sole purpose of being able to consume a broader range of literature, but I couldn't imagine why someone would feel the need to pen a book about Hell in French or Spanish.

Moreover, the entire point of the pits was that very few made it out of there, let alone with the desire to write about their experience afterward. There weren't many resources to pull from.

Finally choosing to accept the small bundle of knowledge, I scooped up the materials and wandered deep into the south side of the library. After fifteen minutes of searching, I was able to locate the red sofa Elijah mentioned, tucked underneath a massive arched window of stained glass. Sinking down into the fleece upholstery, I marveled at how such an ugly piece of furniture could be so comfortable and then opened up the first book the library offered me.

It was titled *A Thousand Cursed Locations*. From haunted cemeteries in the mortal realm to demon-infested temples in the world of the gods, the book was written like a tourist's handbook, though I doubted if it was possible to visit any of the places the author mentioned.

The book was organized alphabetically. I found what I was looking for in the *H* section.

Hell, Darkest Pits, was printed at the top of the page in a modern font.

KNOWN TO BE ONE OF THE MOST TERRIFYING PLACES IN the definable universe, the darkest pits of Hell, located approximately seven thousand miles below the God of the Underworld's famous palace. Constructed several hundred thousand years B.C.E., the pits were intended to be the eternal prison for the King of Hell's first wife, the demon Lilith. Over time, however, it became a convenient dumping ground for various immortal criminals.

Little can be said for certain about the aesthetics of the pits themselves. Many scholars have theorized that they bear a resemblance to the pits of Hell reserved for mortal souls in the kingdoms of Arrogance, Corruption, Disgrace, Savagery, Greed, and Jealousy. If this is true, the darkest pits of Hell are cold, desolate, and chilling to witness. Still, one can assume that a prison meant to contain immortal beings would have to be much more intense than prisons designed for mere mortals.

There's only one way to find out... descend into the darkness and live to tell the tale.

I turned the page, but it was the beginning of a new article titled *Hell, Dark Gardens of Arrogance.*

"Useless," I muttered, hoping the library could hear me. "I learned absolutely nothing knew from that."

The library had nothing to say for itself, so I tossed the book aside and reached for the one whose cover reminded me of tea.

Maybe this was stupid. I was looking for information about a place that was purposefully shrouded in mystery. That's what made it such a good prison. For example, if the details about it were hazy at best, nobody would be able to mastermind a strategy for breaking the prisoners out.

It wasn't right. I refused to accept that Rose belonged down there. Sure, she committed adultery by loving a man who wasn't her betrothed, and she betrayed multiple people by running away from the Underworld, but it's not like she killed anyone. Her actions didn't hurt anyone, at least not physically. In fact, given how swiftly Prince Finn moved on to her twin, I'd say that his emotional wounds from being jilted at the altar were fairly shallow.

Then again, injuring the God of the Underworld's pride was an unwise crime to commit.

Rose accepted her brutal punishment too easily. She didn't protest once. At her trial, she barely lifted her eyes from the ground. It was nauseating to witness. Sasha, the youngest, nearly had a panic attack right there in her seat, all while Rose allowed herself to be dragged away to a doom she didn't deserve.

Rose was like that, though. Rose was always the victim of her own story. Firstborn and inhumanly beautiful, she could've been the most powerful demigoddess to come from a minor god, but she wasn't built to withstand that kind of pressure. She caved under the spitefulness of her twin. Riven was different than her. Instead of being victimized by her second-born status, she asserted herself as the villain in everyone's story but her own.

Not that it was Riven's fault that Rose was being punished for falling in love, but... I digress.

With a huff, I opened the next book.

Creatures of Hell, it was called.

Despite its brevity, it covered many different animals native to the Underworld—blood-sucking eels in the Red River, mail carrier crows, hellhounds, and several species of snakes. I skimmed the pages but didn't find anything about the darkest pits of Hell.

"Useless again," I told the library.

The third book, bound in smooth leather, seemed promising. It was a handwritten journal penned by a mortal psychologist from the Underworld who interviewed a prisoner that actually made it out of the darkest pits. Apparently, the prisoner was a demigod named Maurice, the son of Tempest, who was the goddess of deceit, and my father's newest enemy. According to the scribbled journal entries, he was imprisoned approximately three hundred years ago for a century, punishment delivered after he was so taken with the God of the Underworld's wife

Raya that he dove into the Red River and attempted to woo her.

Raya wanted to kill the demigod, but Tempest pleaded for her son's mercy, wrote the psychologist. *In the end, the God of the Underworld convinced his wife to accept one hundred years in the darkest pits of Hell for his blasphemous flirtations.*

Unfortunately, that was about as interesting as the journal's content got. The psychologist spent dozens of pages describing the tortured demigod's ragged appearance but wasn't able to get many words out of him. Apparently, after a century in the pits, Maurice wasn't capable of more than a stuttered string of mumbles and wordless trembles.

That wasn't what I wanted to read.

"She's down there," Maurice tells me each time we speak. "She's real. She's down there, but she knows how to get out." It has taken me weeks to prod more details out of him, but when he finally uttered a name, it was obvious and unsatisfying.

"Lilith," he clarified. "Lilith is down there, but she knows all that occurs up here." Clearly, the demigod has been driven mad by his imprisonment. It is common knowl-

edge that the prison in the darkest pits was constructed for Lilith and that, therefore, the demon is down there. In terms of Maurice's fears that Lilith can escape, I have decided to write this off as the paranoid musings of a half-mortal with very little will to live left in him.

THAT WAS CREEPY, TO SAY THE LEAST.

With a forlorn sigh, I finished reading the journal entries. The ending of Maurice's story was horribly depressing. Apparently, he never recovered from his time in the darkest pits of Hell. Tempest tried to heal her son, but she was a minor goddess with little powers outside of wicked deceitfulness. Nobody wanted to cross the God of the Underworld, so she was denied help by all others.

Eventually, when Maurice's demigod life was in its twilight, he went to the mortal realm and threw himself into an active volcano to meet death on his own terms.

I slammed the journal shut. Agitation set my nerves on fire. I fought the urge to throw the books at the wall. The Library of the Underworld was supposed to be helpful. It was supposed to have all the answers.

No, it isn't, I reminded myself in an attempt to

calm down. *It doesn't have all the answers, just the ones that were written down into books.*

I reached for the wooden cylinder and yanked off the stopper. A role of thin paper came out. Desperate for something useful, I unraveled it and lay it flat on the nearest table.

Map of the Darkest Pits of Hell was written at the top of the paper.

But the rest of the parchment was blank. Whoever had the idea to draw the map of the worst prison ever created never got the chance.

"Oh, my gods," I growled, pressing my palms to my face. "Please get this nonsense out of my sight."

When I took a deep breath and let my hands drop to my sides a moment later, I noticed that the library had obeyed me. The books and the unfinished map were gone, sucked back up into the sky when I wasn't looking.

I flopped back onto the couch, feeling like a lousy excuse for an intellectual. I'd never had such a difficult time doing research before, not even when I didn't have the Library of the Underworld at my disposal.

I didn't want to give up, but it seemed like the library didn't have anything else to offer me in terms of a thorough description of what Rose was suffering through. Wasn't there something I could do?

No, there wasn't. I was being ridiculous. Nobody could go against the law of the God of the Underworld.

I lay on the red couch, staring up into the abyss of knowledge, and lost track of time. Only when a distant clock chimed that it was noon did I sit up and face the shelves with fresh determination.

If the library didn't have anything to tell me about Rose's prison, that was fine. I wasn't giving up but rather temporarily putting the research on hold in hopes that I would come up with a better question to ask the library. There had to be some way to unlock the truth, some kind of roundabout roster of inquiries that could help me piece together the darkest pits of Hell.

Hey, library, I thought to myself. *Do you have any*

note-taking supplies? Perhaps a blank journal I could have?

A few seconds later, a dark purple journal with a suede cover and a fresh fountain pen flopped onto the cushion beside me.

"Thanks," I muttered. I was confident that I was still as alone as ever in the library. Understandably, I was the only person in the palace who was in the mood for studying the day after my wedding.

I flipped to the first page of the journal and scribbled down the physical descriptions of the books I'd looked at, alongside a basic summary of its contents. I had a decent memory, but I didn't want to risk losing track of my research when the topic was this personal.

Then, I turned to the next page. The tip of the pen hovered over the smooth paper. I drew the number two at the top. To anyone else who might get their hands on my new journal, they might think I was simply notating the page number, but I knew what it really stood for.

2, as in the second daughter… as in Riven.

Rose wasn't the only sister I couldn't stop thinking about. My encounter with Riven last night on the balcony puzzled me, and I had a feeling that there was something I was forgetting, a deep sense of foreboding that was impossible to explain.

Okay, library, I said internally, closing my eyes like the first time. *I forgive you for not giving me much about the pits. That was my fault, and I'll figure it out. Until then, can you tell me the symptoms of a psychotic breakdown?*

Instantly, I knew I should've remembered Elijah's warning. Hundreds of books tumbled to the floor, old and new, forming a mountain of tomes dedicated to the study of psychosis over the centuries. The stream of books continued, tumbling down from the sky, a few of them narrowly missing my head.

"Wait, stop," I snapped, holding up my hands. The waterfall of books didn't stop at my command, so I quickly thought of a new question. "How do I know if someone is losing their grip on reality?"

Before my eyes, the stream of books reversed as the library lifted half the volumes that were irrelevant to my revised inquiry back up to their respective shelves. However, their numbers were swiftly replaced by a fresh pile of more philosophy-based guides. I was left with hundreds of books to sort through.

I tried not to curse at the library. It was trying to

help me, and it was my fault that I couldn't ask a decent question.

I remembered the way Riven's body locked up on the day of Rose's trial, her muscles tense and her face frozen with fear as she stared at her bare arm. Only her eyes moved, trailing from her wrist to her hand and then all the way down to the ground before she slowly relaxed and returned to her normal self as if nothing had happened in the first place.

Then, again, on the balcony, she was still as stone and visibly unnerved, though the terror was less obvious than the first time around. Still, she recovered just as quickly last night as she did in the God of the Underworld's temporary courtroom.

How do I know if someone is hallucinating? I asked.

The library recalled two-thirds of the psychology texts, leaving me with a pile more comparable to a hill than a mountain. Resigned to accept that I merely had multiple perspectives to learn from, I grabbed the first book I laid eyes on and rested it on my knees. It was thick and heavy, the front covered in a transparent film. From the photographs printed on the cover, I could tell that it was a textbook for a school in the mortal realm.

Psychology 101, it was titled. I flipped to the table of contents, located the page where the chapter on psychological disorders began, then skimmed until I found the subsection labeled *Symptoms of Psychosis*, and finally got to a paragraph detailing the signs and causes of hallucinations.

Hallucinations can occur via all five senses. Individuals can see, hear, touch, smell, and taste things that have no basis in reality. The most common forms of hallucinations are auditory and visual.

"Can you see it, too?" Riven had asked me. "Can you hear it?"

I couldn't see or hear anything other than the normal noises of the night that surrounded us, so it seemed logical to conclude that Riven was witnessing something that wasn't real, that only existed in her mind.

I continued reading.

Hallucinations can be a symptom of various different mental and physical disorders. Diagnosis typically involves blood tests, checking for abnormal electrical activity in the brain, and various forms of imaging scans.

.   .   .

THE SMALL PARAGRAPH WAS FOLLOWED BY A LONG LIST of health conditions that a demigoddess would likely never suffer from. I tossed the textbook back in the pile.

"Is there anything you can tell me specifically about people with divine blood who experience hallucinations?" I grumbled.

The library recalled the majority of the books and spat out a few others, leaving me with a neat stack of about twenty to comb through. The first title on the stack was *Psychology of Gods and Goddesses*.

I spent the afternoon skimming the books for information. Some of it was helpful, such as a research study that showed some half-mortals could develop psychological disorders previously thought to be exclusive to mortals, but only in extremely rare cases. Another author noted that it was common for people to mistake divine signals as hallucinations. Historically, gods weren't always clear in their messaging, so that made sense.

Using the purple journal, I diligently cataloged each book I opened. It was an arduous process, but what else was I going to do? Leave the library, seek out Riven, and ask if she wanted to braid each other's hair?

"What time is it?" I asked the library, no longer caring if I sounded weird for talking out loud. In response, the same chime that I heard at noon rang out four times. It was four in the afternoon. I'd been researching for hours and still wasn't any closer to figuring out what was going on inside Riven's mind.

Maybe she was telling the truth when she told me she was practicing her acting skills, trying to freak me out on purpose with her glassy eyes and ragged whisper. But that didn't explain why it happened the first time. Why would she pull a stunt like that on the day of a public execution and our sister's trial? I doubted she was aware I even noticed her odd behavior, fleeting as it was.

"You can have those back," I muttered, waving my hands at the twenty discarded books. Dutifully, the library claimed them once more. I stared at my journal, tapping the gifted pen against my temple.

Think, Chloe, I urged myself. *You're smarter than this. What other angle can you observe the issue from? Think, think, think.*

I pummeled my brain into submission, desperate to make significant progress before the day was over.

Suddenly, a metaphorical lamp flickered to life in my mind. The answer was so obvious that I wanted to kick myself for being so foolish. The problem wasn't that the library couldn't help me, but rather that I was standing in my own way. Accustomed to the mortal literature I devoured, I'd made the mistake of thinking like a mortal. When I tried to reason through Riven's behavior, I stuck to logic and science, and medicine.

But I was sitting in a library that could understand me as if it was a living person. I was in a palace ruled by a god who reigned over death itself. I was married to an immortal prince who could turn my bones to dust or uproot a giant sequoia with a blink of his eyes... at least after maturing for a few centuries.

I wasn't thinking like a demigoddess. Flipping back through the notes I took, I recalled the book about various creatures that lurked in the Underworld, some benign and others downright malignant.

What if Riven wasn't hallucinating? What if the thing she was seeing and hearing was merely invisible to me?

I cleared my throat and then looked up at the

abundant shelves. I was determined to be specific this time.

"What kind of creatures or beings in the immortal realm can appear visible and audible to a person or people of their choosing, but simultaneously invisible and inaudible to others around them?"

Proud of myself, I waited for the library to respond. For a few minutes, nothing happened. I was immediately worried that the answer to my question was exactly that—nothing—until a familiar book was deposited at my feet. It was the same brown-hued publication I received earlier when I was asking about the darkest pits of Hell—*Creatures of Hell.*

It was followed by exactly seven more books, all relatively short in length.

I got back to work.

Unfortunately, the library couldn't open a book to the right page for me. I had to be more diligent with my skimming, but I slowly came up with a list of possibilities.

First of all, gods and goddesses themselves could choose to be invisible to all but their target. That was obvious. But why would a god need to speak with Riven without revealing themselves to me, and why would they do it while sitting on a branch?

Hellhounds were also an obvious hypothesis, but they were visible only to their victims and demons. However, Riven didn't have any dog bites or claw marks on her flawless skin and, although she wasn't the sweetest, she definitely wasn't a demon.

There were fairies, but they were repelled by the suffering souls of the Underworld and didn't dwell here.

A certain species of butterfly was believed to only be visible to twins, but why would Riven be afraid of a butterfly?

I was just about to turn the next page in the book I was currently working through when a voice startled me out of focus.

"You're like a kid in a candy shop."

I jumped, looking up to find Prince Elijah watching me from the end of the nearest aisle, leaning against a shelf with his hands shoved into the pockets. I had no idea how long he'd been standing there, but the amused look on his face told me he'd likely tried several times to get my attention before I finally snapped out of it.

He looked tired and slightly rumpled. Whatever

matters of state he had to attend to had left their mark.

I smiled and casually closed the journal, hoping that it didn't look too suspicious for me to hide my notes as he approached.

"Is it dinner time already?" I asked.

"Mhm," he said. "What have you been working on?"

Take the books back! I commanded the library. Instantly, the library obeyed, the numerous books shooting upwards as if pulled by a string.

With fast reflexes, Elijah snatched one of the books out of thin air and read the spine.

"*Beasts In the Dark?*" he asked.

I shrugged. "I've recently become interested in zoology."

The second Elijah let go of the book, it zoomed up to the ceiling.

"Really? You're not going to ask if we can get a pet, are you?"

"Would you say no?" I replied.

"Depends on what it is. How about a cat? Cats are nice."

"Let's table this discussion," I suggested, tucking the journal under my arm. "I think we're going to be late for dinner."

I WISHED WE WERE LATE FOR DINNER. I WISHED WE were so late that we missed it entirely. It was an overwhelming affair, with the God of the Under-world at the head of the table, all six of his sons and the remaining five of us sisters seated in order of age and rank. According to the god, he wanted everyone to have dinner together once a week. On all other evenings, we could choose where to join him in the formal dining room or not.

It was pointless, in my opinion. Gods didn't need to eat. Furthermore, no number of dinners would convince any of the siblings seated at the table to get along. Of course, the God of the Underworld wasn't interested in camaraderie. He probably just wanted the excuse to gather everyone in the same place and gauge the success, or lack thereof, of the matches he and Zoren made.

None of the other princes looked as rumpled as Elijah, but I tried not to think too deeply about it. There were other things to fret about.

At least no one expected me to speak. The nobles who lived in the God of the Underworld's court weren't invited to the "family" dinner, and none of the princes or my sisters cared to ask how Elijah and

I were faring now that we'd been married for a full day.

When the God of the Underworld wasn't controlling the conversation, Riven took the reins. She bent over backward to charm those around her, earning a few smiles and comments from the princes and even a few stubborn chuckles from the younger sisters. Prince Finn sat back and let her take the lead, clearly amused by her chatter. It seemed like they got over their disgruntlement at the new living arrangements easily enough.

I didn't say a word, nor did Elijah. We ate quietly, minding our manners but otherwise not contributing to the conversation. It was normal for us to dwell within our own heads even while we were sharing a meal. In the palace of Disgrace, nobody would've thought twice about it, used to their prince's demeanor and accepting of my similar conduct.

There was one other person at the table who had his lips completely sealed. He didn't open his mouth even to take a sip of wine.

Prince Nico of Corruption gracefully conceded to his older brother when it was announced that Riven would marry Finn instead of him, but that was because he was in public. With no one to witness his bad attitude but his father, his brothers, and five inconsequential demigoddesses, Nico wore his heart on his sleeve.

To make matters worse, he was sitting on his father's left, directly across from Finn and Riven. With only Elijah between the surly prince of Corruption and me, I was able to observe him very closely.

He looked downright murderous, his hands clenched in his lap and his jaw firmly set. It looked as if he was trying very hard to control his emotions. Did he have a temper? I hoped I wouldn't find out.

While Riven bubbled over with charisma and elegance, Nico stewed in his frustration. I never dared to ask, but I'd managed to overhear a gaggle of gossiping nobles from Corruption at Riven's wedding reception mention that, at one point time, she and Nico were obviously smitten.

So, Riven broke his heart, and now she was laughing in his face.

Prince Finn's gaze slid right past Nico as if he wasn't really there. Even the God of the Underworld, who could read our minds if he wanted to, chose to ignore his son's obvious anger. I found it difficult to be on their side, though it was expected of me. Naturally, it made sense for the God of the

Underworld to make his eldest son's marriage a priority. He was the heir to his throne, and he needed a queen so that he could have heirs of his own and a loyal partner to rule by his side. In Rose's absence, Riven stepped up as the most favorable option.

Logically, I understood it. Our father disowned Rose as soon as he heard she ran away, so Riven technically became the firstborn. She was also confident, self-assured, and unflinchingly bold, where Rose was meek, mild, and compliant. Admittedly, Riven seemed suited to leadership in the Underworld.

And yet... to take your second son's betrothed and give her to your firstborn seemed wildly unfair. Nico had likely spent most of his life watching Finn win the majority of the favor from his parents just because he had the luck of blooming into divine existence first.

Then, to make that second-born prince sit at the same dinner table as his older brother and his former lover—it was cruel.

That's what it was. They were all cruel. They were villains.

Suddenly, I couldn't stomach the preposterous scene any longer. I put down my knife and fork, then pressed the back of my hand to my forehead, forcing my eyelids to flutter weakly.

Prince Declan, sitting right across the table from me, was the first to notice. He grinned wolfishly.

"Oldest trick in the book," he muttered, causing both his future wife Amalia and Elijah to glance up in confusion. Without acknowledging them, Declan cleared his throat and addressed the God of the Underworld. "Father, don't you think we've forced the newlyweds to socialize for long enough? Princess Chloe looks weary, and surely my brother would like to be alone with his new wife?"

I wanted to kick him under the table, though his lewd commentary was undeniably helpful. While silence fell and all eyes shifted toward me and my weak attempt at feigning exhaustion, I squirmed uncomfortably.

The God of the Underworld chuckled.

"Silly me," he said. "Where is my head? Elijah and Chloe, please feel free to retire. All others, kindly stay for a little while longer."

The end of his statement seemed directed at Nico, but the god didn't glance at his son once while saying it. My victory was mixed with guilt as I was freed from the table, standing with Elijah, and leaving the dining room without delay. If only the

God of the Underworld extended the dismissal to the rest of the dinner table, then Nico could excuse himself to quell his anger in private.

Sorry, I wanted to tell the second prince. I tried.

CHAPTER 7

"I don't think I've ever been grateful that Declan opened his mouth and decided to speak before," Elijah pondered once we were back in our suite in the east wing. "I suppose there's a first time for everything."

My agitation had returned, fueled by the discomfort in the dining room. I paced back and forth in front of the bed while Elijah sank down onto the chaise.

"Sorry," I told him, wringing my hands. "That was just… overwhelming."

"Yes, it was," Elijah agreed. "I was convinced Nico was about to set the tablecloth on fire."

"I simply can't believe he's being forced to still

participate in all of this without a betrothal," I replied, rubbing my temples. Prince Nico wasn't the true source of my frustration, but he was the channel I was choosing to pour all of my negative emotions into for the moment. "It almost seems like a punishment."

Elijah shrugged. "I thought so too, but I think it must be because our father is coordinating potential new matches for him."

I paused in my pacing, praying I sounded reasonably casual when I asked, "Did your father mention that in your meeting today?"

"Hmm?" Elijah seemed confused by my question and then apparently remembered the excuse he gave me when we parted ways that morning. "Oh, right. No, he didn't. We discussed… other things."

His avoidant behavior did nothing to suppress my general feelings of vexation. Talking to Elijah felt like talking to the library. I could ask them both whatever I wanted, but neither would give me a precise, clear answer. I didn't have the patience to dissect Elijah like those books, so instead of asking for details on the *other things* my husband talked about with the god who imprisoned my sister, controlled our fates, and played with us like pawns on a chessboard, I stomped into the bathroom.

After changing into a more modest nightgown than the one hung up for me the night prior, I returned to the bedroom and crawled right into bed without a word. Elijah was sitting in the same spot, brow furrowed as he tried to determine the reason for my moodiness.

Leaving him to his thoughts, I threw the covers over my head and willed my brain to stop its whirring and whizzing so that sleep could become a possibility before sunrise. Then, to my surprise, the mattress sank beside me as Elijah sat down on my side of the bed, mere inches from my recumbent body.

I peeked over the top of the covers, quirking an eyebrow at him.

"Are you alright?" he asked.

"I..." I didn't know how to answer the question. Very few people throughout my life had bothered to ask me something like that.

I couldn't be truthful with Elijah, though. I couldn't tell him that I was so worried about Rose that I desperately dug for details to convince myself that her prison wasn't as bad as the legends claimed, only to discover that it was much worse than I was capable of imaging... so terrible that a demigod threw himself into a volcano to end the misery that clung to him even after being released.

I also couldn't tell him about Riven. He didn't know my sister as I did. He had no evidence to prove that she couldn't crumble under the stress of becoming the future Queen of Hell and start hallucinating disturbing images. Nor did he know that, of all the invisible monsters that crawled through the Underworld, Riven was not the kind of person who would ever be considered easy prey.

I supposed I could mention that I was concerned about Nico's anger, but it seemed like a frivolous side quest that could wait for another day.

In truth, I should just learn to mind my business. If I was like Riven and thought of nobody but myself, I'd be less anxious.

"I'm fine," I lied to Elijah. "Just tired."

He nodded quietly. I could tell he knew that I wasn't being completely truthful.

"I understand this is all very weird, but I was serious yesterday when I told you that I would really appreciate a friendship with you," he said. "Perhaps it's an unconventional friendship, considering that we sleep in the same bed, but that's not quite so terrible, is it?"

Elijah seemed genuinely worried that I was going to contradict him and inform him that sharing a bed that could fit ten other people in it with him was the worst torture known to mankind. I softened.

"No, it's not," I admitted. "I can think of worse things to endure."

He chuckled. "That's a relief."

I waited for him to say something else or to stand up and move to his respective side of the mattress, but he remained where he was and fiddled with his hands in his lap. He had more to tell me, but words were evading him. I sat up and reached out for his shoulder to… well, I didn't know. Pat him encouragingly? Poke him playfully and lighten the mood? I was dizzy from the day I'd had and didn't know what to do with all of my varying emotions.

"Are you—" I began, but Elijah didn't hear me and started speaking all of a sudden.

"I know we didn't talk much before when we were engaged, and you were settling into life in Disgrace, but it wasn't because I didn't like you or didn't want your company," he said, continuing to look at his hands. "It's just that you made me nervous—"

"I made you nervous? Have you seen me?" I

laughed, blissfully distracted from my earlier frustrations.

Elijah blushed and met my inquiring eyes. "Yes, and that is exactly the source of my frayed nerves. You're so pretty and so clearly smarter than me, both of which were alarming and alluring at the same time. I don't know…"

"Oh."

"And I'm not very good with words. I say dumb things and usually make a fool of myself. I'm not eloquent, not like my brothers. People think that, because I read a lot, I should be well-spoken, but they don't take into account that those who read a lot are inclined to prefer it over any other form of communication."

I couldn't stop the smile from spreading across my face.

"You sound incredibly well-spoken right now, if that helps," I told him.

"Well, I practiced this speech, so it doesn't count," he confessed with a breath of laughter.

"I get it," I replied. "I'm the same way. People always assumed that reading a ton of books meant that I was also a writer, but I'm actually terrible at it. I can't create. I can only appreciate what has already been created."

Elijah nodded. "See? We have a lot in common. I would've known this so much sooner if I had the guts to speak to you from the beginning."

"Better late than never," I said. "Anyway, I was shy around you for the same reasons. You know, the handsomeness and the intellect… I think I was worried that you wouldn't see me as a worthy partner."

"Nonsense," Elijah gasped. "If anyone is lacking, it's me."

I shook my head, but I could tell this wasn't something that we were going to agree on. The problem with being studious *and* humble at the same time was that you were rarely willing to acknowledge your merit, especially in comparison to others.

A sudden yawn escaped me, causing Elijah to leap up from the bed.

"I'll let you get some sleep," he muttered, hurrying away into the bathroom. His shyness ebbed and flowed, a modesty that was difficult to predict.

I could get used to him, though. I already liked him. Despite his small lies and moments of evasion, I wanted to trust him. Further down the road, I could see my fondness for Elijah growing into something stronger than friendship. Perhaps one day, we could truly be in love. We just needed time and, luckily, we would have all the time in the world.

Closing my eyes, I fell asleep with a mind devoid of worry about my unanswered questions and full of thoughts about the pretty gold glints in Elijah's eyes.

However, when I woke up the next morning, he was already gone.

Sitting up in confusion, I looked out the windows and saw that the sun was just barely over the horizon. It was dawn. Even though I'd been the one to wake up before him yesterday, Elijah's side of the bed was empty. Blinking sleep from my eyes, I reached out and patted the rumpled sheets. They were still warm; it hadn't been long since he got up.

The bathroom door was open, the interior silent. I stood and poked my head through the doorway to confirm he wasn't in there, then shuffled to the parlor to see if he was puttering around in his study.

But he was completely gone. He didn't even leave a note. It was as if the conversation we had the night before about communicating with each other never happened. Feeling disappointed and regretful, I took my wounded pride and got dressed for the day. As I was tying my hair back in a knot, I heard the main door to our suite opening and closing. Thinking that it was Elijah and rapidly concluding that he surely had a good reason for leaving me to wake up alone on my second day in an unfamiliar palace, I hurried toward the reception chamber.

A familiar figure entered the room, but it wasn't Elijah.

"Milou?" I asked, taking in the sight of the girl who was my maid in the palace of Disgrace. Her soft, freckled features molded into a pleasant smile as she dipped into a curtsy. "What are you doing here?"

Before she could answer, another figure appeared at her side. It was Zak, Elijah's personal attendant from Disgrace. He was blond and fair like my maid; I once asked if they were siblings, but they laughed and told me they weren't related. I supposed I couldn't help assuming that everyone had as many siblings as I did.

"The God of the Underworld sent for us, madam," explained Zak, sweeping into a respectful bow. "We arrived only an hour ago."

"When we learned that you would be staying here for a year, we were worried that we had lost our positions," Milou whispered. "But when we received word that the God of the Underworld was summoning us to attend to you for the duration of your stay, I was so honored."

"We brought some things that you and his Highness might enjoy having from home," Zak added. "Books, mostly."

I grinned. I didn't think I would feel so relieved to see the familiar servants. Milou was gentle and polite, but she also wasn't afraid of chatter, likely because she felt the need to fill the silence where I chose not to speak out of habit.

"I'm very happy to see both of you," I told them. "I hope the journey was okay?"

They nodded in unison.

"I haven't left Disgrace since I was a little girl," Milou admitted. "It was very exciting."

Fidgeting with my skirts, I glanced around the room. My plan had been to go back to the library and distract myself from Elijah's unknown whereabouts, but maybe Zak could tell me.

"I know you just arrived," I said to him. "But would you happen to know where the prince is?"

"Yes, madam. I saw him in the grand hall downstairs. He said he wouldn't be at the palace today, but he'd be back in the evening," Zak answered. "He also warned us that you would likely already be in the library by the time we came upstairs, but it seemed we were just a few minutes too quick for you."

He smiled brightly. I tried to answer it in kind.

"Right," I said. Did he think it was weird that I didn't know where my own husband was? "Well, I should excuse myself. Please get some rest. There isn't much work for you to do at the moment."

"We'll keep ourselves busy," Milou promised, curtsying as I tucked my journal under my arm, slipped from the room, and walked briskly down the hallway.

Elijah had left the palace. It didn't occur to me that we could do that. Of course, the God of the Underworld said that we were obliged to live here, but that didn't mean we couldn't leave the palace during the day. Not that I had anywhere to go. Disgrace was so far away that, even if I left before sunrise, I would have to turn around and go back by the time I made it there in order to return to the God of the Underworld's central city before dinnertime.

Why did Elijah leave the palace? Was he in the city? Wandering the villages that sprawled out far and wide before dissolving into the separate territory owned by the six princes? Why would he do that without me?

Stop whining, I chastised myself. *Neediness isn't charming. Elijah doesn't have to take you with him everywhere.*

Maybe the God of the Underworld and his sons had matters to attend to elsewhere, routine godly duties that my sisters and I weren't privy to while we were still half-mortal. Even in that case, however, it would've been nice for Elijah to mention it when we were talking after dinner.

On my way to the library, I passed a parlor where I spotted Sasha and Danai having a surprisingly early breakfast. I slipped past before they could notice me. Amalia usually skulked around in corners, so I doubted I would run into her, and Riven only appeared when she wanted something from you—whether tears, blood, or praise—so I didn't run the risk of seeing anyone but my youngest sisters.

Were their princes also missing this morning? Did my sisters get an explanation?

My frustration levels were peaking again, rising quickly to match the agitation I felt yesterday. Unable to bear the mystery any longer, I stopped the first servant who walked past me.

"Excuse me," I said to him as his eyes widened

and he quickly sank into a bow. "Is the God of the Underworld in the palace this morning?"

The servant seemed confused by my question, frowning as if the answer should've been obvious.

"Of course, madam," he replied. "He does not leave often."

I nodded. "And the other princes? Are they here, too?"

The servant shrugged. "I believe so, yes. Most of them are still asleep, but I have seen his Highness Prince Finn in the throne room with his wife."

What were they doing in there? Especially at this hour…

I sighed. That was another question to add to the list.

"What about Prince Elijah?" I pressed. Over the past few months, I gathered from Milou that servants in the Underworld were more attuned to their royals. They were expected to be aware of our comings and goings, even if they didn't personally attend to us.

The servant shook his head. "His Highness ordered a carriage at sunrise. I believe he is gone for the day, madam."

"Do you know why?" I asked, lowering my voice. Undoubtedly, my questions sounded odd. Interrogating a random servant about the location of various gods wasn't normal.

"No, madam," the servant said. "I am sorry."

"It's okay," I responded quickly. "Thank you."

Feeling like a fool, I bustled away from the servant and traced the path that Elijah and I took to the library yesterday morning. However, when I arrived in the mystical expanse of knowledge, I found myself more puzzled than ever before. Sinking into the familiar red couch, I stared up at the ceiling.

Elijah was the only prince who left the palace today. Everyone else, including his father, was here. He didn't bother to tell me why he left, but he'd been spotted by at least three servants willingly getting into a carriage and leaving the grounds, so it wasn't as if the young god was kidnapped. To consider the possibility was preposterous.

Does the third son of the God of the Underworld have any special duties that the other sons don't, which he must tend to alone and in secret? I asked the library.

The deafening silence and stillness that followed told me everything I needed to know. There was no easy answer for why I woke up alone that morning. Despite the fact that I'd been warming up to him and even had the confidence to tell him that I thought he was handsome, my tentative trust in Prince Elijah was rapidly waning.

He was, after all, the prince of Disgrace. Didn't that mean he was inclined to be disgraceful himself?

What is he up to? I wondered more to myself than the boundless shelves.

The library stayed quiet.

CHAPTER 8

*F*ine, I snapped at the library, glaring up at the ceiling as if it had eyes that could see the annoyed expression on my face. *Scratch that. Can you give me what I was reading before Elijah interrupted me yesterday?*

Soon enough, a dozen books dropped from the sky and skittered to a halt at my feet in a disorganized heap.

"Thanks," I grumbled, stooping to stack them up and carry them over to the table beside the red couch. Then, I opened up my journal to the most recent page and went through my notes from yesterday.

Before Elijah showed up to collect me for dinner, I was in the middle of researching Hellish beings that could choose who saw and heard them even within a crowded room. So far, I'd ruled out other gods and goddesses, hellhounds, fairies, and creepy butterflies.

I sighed loudly and nestled back deep into the cushions, grabbing *Beasts in the Dark* and flipping to the last page I remembered reading. I seriously hoped I was on the right track. I was a diligent student, but I didn't know how much longer I could go on throwing guesses out into the dark.

The next chapter in the book was about ghosts and other various specters in the shadows. The Underworld was full of the souls of the dead. In fact, the suffering of the sinful was what fueled the powerful realm, what kept the Red River flowing, and what maintained the God of the Underworld's dominance over other immortal beings. Despite that, it didn't seem likely that there would be ghosts roaming around. It was impossible for a mortal's anguished soul to escape the pits of Hell, and, even if they did manage it, they would crumble into nonexistence within seconds. They were too fragile, too unstable to withstand Hell. Even the mortals who were born here and the immortals who dwelled here struggled to survive the overwhelming darkness of the God of the Underworld.

Anyway, why would a ghost be haunting Riven specifically? We didn't know any dead mortals or demigods. Unless one of her mother's mortal relatives had died and been sent to the Underworld for whatever crimes they might have committed—and, in which case, Riven would never have had the opportunity to know them in the first place—there was nobody who had cause to stalk Riven in their ghostly form.

That was the thing. The six of us sisters had our mothers, but we had no one else to call family except the father we shared and the stepmother who hated us. When our mothers became pregnant, Zoren brought them to his kingdom, stealing them away from the lives they had in the mortal world. Furthermore, they were discouraged from discussing it with us. My own mother shared a few tidbits of her life, like the city she was from, the career she had, and small details here and there in general about the world from which she came.

In my life, I'd said about ten words to Riven and Rose's mother, but she didn't seem as though she was willing to discuss the mortal realm with anyone, including her daughters. She was the first mistress of Zoren, so she'd been there the longest.

I pinched the bridge of my nose and refocused on

the book in front of me. Clearly, my thoughts were easily distracted today. I blamed it on the new living arrangements. In Disgrace, it didn't take me long to become comfortable and relaxed in the humble, cozy palace. It was quiet and peaceful, and there were no sisters or princes of Hell other than Elijah roaming around. I didn't have to worry about whatever visions Riven was seeing in the dark or where Elijah was disappearing to without telling me. Not to mention the fact that the God of the Underworld was here. Even with his library at my disposal, life here was not something I could see myself settling into.

All I could do was hope for the next year to pass by quickly and uneventfully. My sisters would get married, Nico would find a suitable match, and then we could all part ways, and everything could go back to normal. Or rather, the new normal we were thrust into when our father brought us here in the first place.

Until then, I would keep myself busy by solving a few minor mysteries and gaining knowledge. That's what I valued most in life. Knowledge.

I shifted positions and tucked my feet underneath my body, propping my elbow up on the arm of the couch and turning the page.

But, as I continued reading, there was nothing helpful leaping out at me. The creatures that I read about were frightening enough to cause Riven to react as terrified as I'd seen her do, but they didn't have the ability to turn invisible. Werewolves, gorgons, and basilisks... they'd never be able to threaten my sister without me seeing them, too.

I paused and glanced up at the towering shelves. Was there a chance that there was something wrong with *me*? After twenty years of reading all hours of the day, was I experiencing some kind of selective sight loss? Could it be that the reason I had no idea what was plaguing Riven was because I couldn't see clearly enough in the first place?

But no. The first time I noticed Riven's strange reaction to an unseen occurrence, it was broad daylight. We were sitting under the sun in the courtyard, and we had just watched a boy die.

Furthermore, if I had sight problems, so did everyone else in the crowd. Nobody else noticed the way Riven tensed up and stared at her wrist as if it was suddenly on fire or turning to stone before her eyes. Not a single one of the powerful gods who sat around us sensed anything afoot.

No. I wasn't the crazy one. I couldn't be.

I tossed the book aside and reached for the next

one. However, as I opened it to the first page, I felt an overwhelming sense of dread. I was on the verge of giving up. Why did I care so much anyway? Riven could deal with her own problems. She was the one who took our new positions here way too far, reaching for the stars—Prince Finn—as soon as the opportunity arose. If she was experiencing bad karma for that, I should probably mind my business.

Slamming the book shut, I shoved it off my lap and onto the cushion beside me.

Can't you just tell me what's wrong with my sister? I asked the library. *Surely you know she's here in the palace, considering there's probably a list of current guests somewhere in your recent archives, and surely you can see into her head the same way you can see into mine?*

The library spat out a scroll. I snatched it from midair, unraveling it greedily only to discover that it was, in fact, a list of current guests at the palace. My sisters and I were written at the top of the list in curling, sophisticated script, followed by dozens more. I recognized Milou and Zak's names, so I figured the unfamiliar names were the servants who came from the separate kingdoms to attend to us for the next year.

"Thank you," I sighed, rolling the parchment back up. "That's not really what I was asking for, though."

The library sucked the parchment out of my hands. I frowned at my empty palm, held aloft as if waiting for something else that wouldn't come. I was growing more confident in my belief that

I know you only have published books or official documents, but what about mail? Notes passed between secret messengers? What's your definition of 'published'? It's got to be broader than what you've been suggesting.

There was an odd creak from overhead as if the library was sighing at me for questioning it.

Then, with a strange fluttering noise that reminded me of wings, something floated down toward my waiting palm. It wasn't a book, nor was it another roll of parchment or even a letter.

It was bright red and light as a feather, so delicate that it wafted down with weightless leisure and forced me to be patient as it came into view. Whether a scrap of fabric or a piece of string, it glimmered in the rays of light that passed through the stained-glass window behind me.

When it finally landed in the palm of my waiting hand, I realized it was a ribbon. Scarlet satin, woven with a high-quality loom—the kind of item only royals could afford.

What is this? I asked the library.

It was quiet.

I tried to figure out which one of my questions the ribbon was supposed to be the answer to as I relaxed back onto the couch and fingered the soft material. I started out by asking the library outright what was wrong with my sister, but then I foolishly asked a handful of follow-up questions, not all of them related.

What was it trying to tell me? Was this a clue?

The red ribbon looked like the sort of thing a child would tie in their hair, but it seemed too short for that purpose. One end of it was flawlessly seamed, but the other end was slightly frayed as if carelessly chopped from a longer length of ribbon. It was also slightly wrinkled at the edges as if it had been working hard to keep something together. I had the feeling that the scrap of ribbon was for utility, not mere decoration.

I gasped aloud.

"Of course," I breathed.

It was the ribbon from a ballet shoe. And I only knew one ballerina personally.

I'd heard rumors of the ballet Riven danced at the palace of Arrogance. It was in the first weeks of Rose's disappearance, long before they had gathered the clues that eventually led to the capture of her and her lover. The only princes in attendance at the performances were Finn and Nico. None of my sisters were invited.

However, people talked—even the humble nobles at Disgrace. They whispered about her blood-red costume and the fearlessness with which she threw her graceful body across the stage. Of course, I'd seen Riven dance before. I knew it was nothing short of miraculous, as cold-hearted as she was.

She wore red when she danced that ballet for Finn. Red, not to symbolize blood or passion or love, but red, the color of Prince Finn's royal house. Riven was clever; even I had to admit it.

But I still didn't know what the ribbon of her ballet shoe had to do with what was causing her to stare into space with sheer terror in her eyes, nor could I explain how the library managed to get ahold of it. There was nothing written on it. It certainly wasn't a published manuscript of anything except my older sister's cunning.

Frowning, I tucked the ribbon into the back of the journal and decided to puzzle over it later. I was just about to reach for the next book in the waiting pile on the table when a voice cracked like a whip through the silence.

"What are you doing?"

I startled and twisted around to see Riven

emerging from within an aisle nearby. My stomach flipped nervously. Had she seen me with the ribbon? Did she know that I was trying to figure her out?

No. The disdain in her eyes was of its usual flavor; she was barking at me because she hated me, not because she was suspicious of me.

I pursed my lips at her as she approached the sofa, her arms crossed against her chest.

"I'm reading, Riven," I replied. "What else would I be doing in a library?"

"This library is creepy," she remarked, wrinkling her nose at the books I'd collected. "Looks like you've picked out a lot of reading material. Are you bored? I guess if my husband was running away from the palace early in the morning, I'd have to find something to occupy myself with, too."

I rolled my eyes at her. Of course, she knew Elijah was gone. She probably had the gossiping servants feeding palace secrets into her ear.

"Perhaps your memory is failing you," I sniffed. "Because I have always been a frequent visitor of libraries."

"Whatever," Riven scoffed, glancing around at the shelves that kept going and going up into the unsee-able distance above her. "How are you supposed to find anything in here anyway?"

Only then did I realize that Riven didn't seek me out to bother me.

She wanted help. She needed to use the library, but she didn't know how. Because she knew me, she assumed I would be in here somewhere and would already know how to make the library deliver its unreachable material to the ground. The problem was, Riven was too proud to ask me point-blank. My sister refused to look weak in front of anyone, least of all one of her siblings.

I snorted and shook my head at her. "What are you looking for?"

Riven narrowed her eyes at me. "Wouldn't you like to know?"

"It's a harmless question," I replied. "I only asked so that I could show you how to make the library work for you."

She pressed her lips together. "I'm not looking for anything, Chloe. It was a rhetorical question."

"Suit yourself," I quipped, looking down at the book in my hands and opening to a random page. It was a signal of dismissal. I waited for Riven to stomp away from me and carry on with her tirade of unpleasantness elsewhere, but she remained still. When I glanced up again, I saw that she was frowning at the shelves with frustration.

"For the love of the gods," I sighed, causing her to whip her face back toward mine. I rolled my eyes at her, understanding that she wasn't going to leave until I gave her what she wanted, even if she was too stubborn to ask me for it.

Hey, library, I thought silently, eyes trained on Riven. *Can you please give me one copy of* Patience? *As in, the fourteenth-century poem from the mortal realm, author unknown?*

Riven glared back at me as my lips curved into a slow smirk.

Within seconds, a thin book dropped onto the arm of the couch with a cheerful *thunk*. I grabbed it and handed it to Riven. She stepped forward and snatched it from me, scoffing when she glanced at the cover.

"What is this?" she snapped.

"Something you should consider reading," I replied. "Then, when you're done with that, I would recommend dabbling in research on the topic of humility. Perhaps kindness, too."

"You're such a freak."

Her insult slid off me uselessly.

"All you have to do is ask the library for what you want, Riven. It's as simple as that. As you saw, you don't even have to ask it out loud."

"You mean, it can read our minds?" she inquired, eyes widening slightly. Was that fear I detected? That was uncharacteristic.

"It seems so," I responded. "Can I be of any further assistance, Your Royal Highness?"

Riven sneered at me, but she didn't respond to my sarcasm. Instead, she chucked *Patience* onto the table and stomped away, satisfied with the information she pried out of me.

With her gone, I decided I'd had enough of thinking about my demonic older sister for the moment. I needed a break. Instead of turning back to the research material I collected, I asked the library for a copy of *Leaves of Grass* by Walt Whitman and lost myself in the peaceful verses of his poetry. It was exactly what my troubled mind needed. Although I'd read the book several times before, it was a comforting sort of familiarity.

After an hour or so, I noticed that I was about to be interrupted again. A shuffling of small but heavy black boots at the end of the nearest row of shelves caught my attention. When I glanced up, I saw my sister Amalia hovering awkwardly in the shadows, biting her lip as she watched me. Unlike Riven, she seemed uncertain about whether or not she wanted to disturb me.

Amalia was only a year younger than me, but that didn't mean we were close. Rather, I preferred to avoid her about as much as Riven. Not because she was just as rude, but because her aura was… eerie. She had long hair that fell in thick tangles around her pale, sallow-cheeked face. Her eyes were unnaturally large, the irises a milky gray. I'd also never seen Amalia smile nor heard her laugh. In short, she was the type of person who probably belonged inside the pages of *Beasts in the Dark*.

She took one step out of the shadows once her cover was blown, her thin hands clasped in front of her. Ever since we were little, Amalia liked to lurk in isolated hiding places. Our father's servants had their work cut out for them, trying to locate her throughout our childhood. It was odd to see her willingly approaching me, especially since there was an entire palace for her to burrow away in until her upcoming wedding day.

"Hi," I said to her, furrowing my brow in confusion.

"Hi," Amalia whispered. Even her voice was hollow and ghostly. "I saw our sister on the other side of the library."

"Oh?" I couldn't recall Amalia ever going out of her way to speak to me.

"She has hundreds of books with her," Amalia told me.

I thought about telling Riven that she needed to be specific with what she asked, but the satisfaction of knowing she would probably get buried under a mountain of useless information was irresistible. It was my small act of revenge for her rudeness.

I nodded, wondering what Amalia's point was. It didn't surprise me that she spied on Riven. She was quiet as a mouse; she probably spied on all of us.

"Okay," I responded. I didn't know what else to say.

Amalia glanced down at her shoes. When she spoke again, her words were directed at them. "They're all about snakes."

I frowned. "Snakes?"

"Yes," Amalia replied. "I've never seen her study before. At least, not about snakes."

"Me either, I guess," I said.

Amalia was looking at me as if she was trying to communicate something with her eyes, but I wasn't catching on. I was too surprised by the fact that she was talking to me in the first place.

"I'll go now," she whispered, ducking her head and scurrying away. I considered calling out after her but couldn't think of anything to say. Instead, I stared at the empty space where she had appeared and then disappeared like a mirage.

How strange. It was one thing for Amalia to be watching our sister from the shadows, but to then seek me out and tell me about what she observed… I was baffled.

Did she notice something weird was going on with Riven, too? Did she know that I was trying to figure it out?

Snakes.

Something tugged at the back of my memory. Regretfully, I set the Whitman book aside and flipped open my notebook.

Snakes, snakes, snakes… Why would Riven be researching something like that unless it was the very thing that was haunting her? But what kind of snake could appear only to its chosen victim?

I received my answer on the third page of the journal, scribbled in the margins next to my notes about Maurice, the demigod who survived his punishment in the darkest pits of Hell only to throw himself into a volcano when he couldn't withstand the torture that followed him even after he was released.

Lilith snake, I wrote. *Connected to Lilith the demon or not?*

It was a question I never revisited, an idle thought that I couldn't remember thinking in the first place. Now, I was certain it was exactly what I was looking for.

I lifted my face to address the library.

"Sorry," I whispered to it. "It seems you already gave me an answer, and I didn't even realize it."

In response, the library coughed up a tiny pamphlet. It fell with a flutter of pages on top of my journal.

Attention to Detail, the pamphlet was titled, followed by a more specific subtitle. *How to Pay Attention and Improve Your Efficiency.*

A bubble of laughter escaped me.

The library had a sense of humor.

CHAPTER 9

The days passed. I woke up to an empty bed, went to the library, and came back to my rooms to pretend to be asleep until Elijah snuck in after dark and slipped into bed. We didn't speak. We barely saw each other.

So much for marital promises and eternal loyalty or whatever. Maybe he regretted opening up to me that night, and this was his way of telling me he wanted to reaffirm the distance between us.

I didn't understand. Last week, we were talking about friendship. Now, we were back to being strangers. It was frustrating, but I had other things to keep me occupied until Elijah finally revealed whatever it was that he was doing when he abandoned me at his father's palace all day long.

I practically lived in the library, though I didn't see Amalia again. Her marriage to Prince Declan was scheduled for next month, so she was likely busy with preparations… or hiding from them.

The day after Amalia offered me the hint about Riven's interest in snakes, and the library sent me a clue in the form of Riven's red ribbon, I became an expert in Lilith snakes. I refreshed myself on the legend of Lilith, the God of the Underworld's first wife. She was a demon and as evil as a creature could be. The darkest pits of Hell were created with the sole purpose of containing her, but many believed that her shapeshifting abilities allowed her rare and fleeting chances for a small part of her to escape.

The Lilith snake was the stuff of nightmares. Much like the demon from which they allegedly came, they were considered a bad omen. According to one of the books the library presented to me, Lilith snakes were often mistaken for hallucinations. Those who were unlucky enough to see them were accused of psychosis and delirium because the snakes could speak without being heard by anyone but their intended target. Similarly, they were selectively invisible.

It explained why I couldn't see whatever was on Riven's arm the day of Rose's trial or whatever was hidden in the branches of the oak tree the night of my wedding. It made sense why Riven got that faraway look in her eyes as if she was listening to a song that nobody else could hear.

Can you see it, too? Can you hear it?

Riven's questions made perfect sense to me now. My sister was haunted by a Lilith snake.

Such an experience was considered a harbinger of doom. Lilith snakes were believed to lead their victims to their downfall, but in a way that the person didn't realize they were cursed until it was too late. Sometimes, the Lilith snakes might even seem like they were bringing you closer to something you desperately wanted. They could also fashion terrible nightmares designed to drive you insane over time.

There were few known victims of Lilith snakes and even fewer books that dared to go into minute detail about the taboo subject of the God of the Underworld's first wife, but I gathered enough research to confirm that Riven was definitely in the process of being led to her doom.

I supposed I was relieved that I couldn't see what she perceived. If the Lilith snake was choosing not to reveal itself to me, it clearly wanted nothing to do with me or my fate.

Perhaps it was cruel of me, but once I solved the mystery of Riven's recent quirks, I couldn't summon much remorse for her. If she was doomed, that was her own fault. She flew too close to the sun, and now she was facing the consequences. If a spooky snake born from an imprisoned demon was messing with her, at least she would be an immortal goddess soon.

I didn't like Riven, but it wasn't as if I wanted her dead.

Armed with the satisfying knowledge of my sister's subtle suffering, I moved on to other topics of research. When I thought about the psychological torture Riven might be enduring at the hands of a Lilith snake, I was immediately reminded of the true torture that her twin was facing while the rest of us enjoyed the comfort of a palace.

Moving on from my study of cursed creatures and frightening beasts, I spent my days having one-sided conversations with the magical library about divine law, governance, and justice.

I'd decided that I was going to help Rose get out of there. One Lilith snake was nothing compared to the demon who resided in the darkest pits of Hell, but if Riven's reaction to the evil serpent was any indication of its sinister ways, I knew that the demon it came from had to be unimaginably worse.

Lilith herself could be whispering horrors into my oldest sister's ear while I slept soundly in my bed every night.

It wasn't right. Rose didn't deserve to be punished in the darkest pits of Hell. She didn't deserve to be treated like a criminal. Her crime was falling in love with the wrong person, but the only reason that poor servant boy was *wrong* was because he wasn't the man that our father arranged for Rose to marry. Yes, she defied Zoren, and she defied the God of the Underworld. She committed adultery against Prince Finn, too. She ran away on her wedding day, enlisting the help of the goddess of runaways to escape without detection. In truth, Rose made many mistakes… but I understood her motivation. I knew my oldest sister was too soft to do anything maliciously. She was the opposite of her twin.

And, despite the poor decisions Rose made while she called the palace of Arrogance home, she didn't deserve to be punished this harshly. I firmly believed that. It was one of the most reckless things I'd ever done, but I'd chosen to disagree with the God of the Underworld.

There had to be something I could do. Even the God of the Underworld had to answer to his own laws. Even the most powerful immortal beings in existence could be persuaded if enough people stood against them in the right way.

Afraid of being found out by Riven—or being spied on by Amalia, whose motivations were still unclear to me—I started carrying thick stacks of books back to the study that had been created for me in the private rooms I shared with Elijah. The library didn't mind relinquishing them; I had a feeling it could reclaim them no matter where I brought the books if it really wanted to. I asked for more journals and more pens, as well as reading glasses to assist with the large amount of dense, fine print and translation materials to decode the Latin and Greek texts that were offered to me.

While the world continued to spin around me and everyone endeavored through journeys of their own, I huddled in my little office in the corner of the palace and trained myself to be a lawyer for my oldest sister. She never asked to be defended, but that didn't mean she didn't deserve to have someone fight for her. Regardless of the fact that we weren't the best of friends, I could no longer stomach the thought of Rose coping with such a fate.

If Maurice, the bold and daring demigod,

couldn't survive the aftereffects of the darkest pits, how could my sweet, timid sister?

I lost myself in my new purpose. If not for my maid Milou, I would forget to eat and drink. I might even forget to bathe and dress. She tended to me, politely prodding me to do something other than bury my head in a mountain of dusty tomes all day, but I resisted her concerns.

After a few days, I nearly forgot about Elijah's absences. I was consumed with swirling thoughts of legal jargon, centuries of godly laws, and summaries of court cases throughout the history of Hell. I crawled into bed with tired eyes and couldn't stay awake to wait for my elusive husband to reappear in the dark.

At least, until one night when I was shaken awake by a warm hand on my shoulder.

I blinked my eyes open to find the lantern on my bedside table lit and a bright fire crackling in the hearth at the end of the room. Elijah was standing over me, his mouth set in a grim line. He was still dressed in his day clothes, though they were rumpled, and the dark shadows under his eyes told me that not even immortals could escape the symptoms of sleep deprivation.

"Chloe, wake up," he whispered. "We need to talk."

"What time is it?" I croaked.

"Midnight."

Scowling at the news that I'd only been asleep for an hour, I sat up and observed Elijah through the dim lighting.

"Did you just get back?" I asked.

He nodded.

"From where?" I ventured.

"That's what we need to discuss," he replied. "What have you been up to while I've been away?"

There was a slightly accusatory note to his voice.

Exhaustion and pent-up frustration built up within me. I threw back the covers and swung my legs over the side of the mattress, my bare feet dangling over the floor. Elijah crossed his arms and took a step back from the bedside.

"You'd already know the answer to that if you weren't gone all day," I hissed. "This is pretty bold of you. You sneak out of the palace before I can wake, then sneak back in after I'm asleep, and you expect me to roll over and provide every detail of my daily life when you ask for it? I am not a blindly obedient wife, Elijah. What happened to us being friends? Friends don't keep secrets."

"Yeah, you're right," he grumbled. "Friends don't keep secrets. That's exactly why I'm starting this discussion, even though all I want to do is go to sleep right now."

"Well, don't let me stop you," I snapped, gesturing to his side of the bed. "I was enjoying some lovely sleep of my own before you decided to become the prince of pointless midnight arguments!"

Elijah exhaled and pinched the bridge of his nose, closing his eyes and shaking his head. I jutted out my chin, confused about how *this* could possibly be our first proper interaction after days of silence.

He cleared his throat and dropped his hand back down to his side.

"I saw your study," he muttered. "I saw the books and your notes—I saw all of it. I wasn't spying, I swear. It's just that I came back and saw that the light was still on in there, so I thought maybe you were still awake. Turns out you just forgot to put out the lantern, so I went inside to take care of it, and that's when I noticed everything on your desk. I didn't know they were accepting demigoddesses into Harvard Law."

Surprised that Elijah even knew about the mortal school of law that I had only just learned about myself, I raised my eyebrows at him.

"Is there something wrong with wanting to study law and politics?" I asked. "Am I not a princess now? Will we not be ruling a kingdom together for the rest of eternity?"

"So, that's what you're up to? You're studying ancient Underworld governance for the purpose of helping me rule a very small, very insignificant kingdom that basically runs itself?" Elijah laughed humorlessly. "Forgive me for being skeptical. Come on, Chloe. I need you to be honest with me. You need to be careful here in my father's house. You can't just—you have to—damnation, can you please just tell me what you're up to?"

A spark of anger flickered to life in my chest. It almost sounded like he had a problem with my becoming a capable leader, even though that excuse was a lie in the first place. I stood up and placed my hands on my hips, glaring up at him. I doubted I looked all that ferocious in my nightgown, not to mention my childish dimples and short stature, but I didn't back down.

"Why don't you tell me what *you're* up to?" I growled.

Elijah pursed his lips at me. "That's not what—"

"No," I interrupted. "Look at you, Elijah. Do you really think you can fool me into thinking you're spending the day being a good little prince when your brothers are still here? Even Prince Finn isn't leaving the palace as often as you. Maybe if you had a wife with a duller mind, you'd be able to fool her, but unfortunately, I'm a little too observant for you to fly under the radar."

"Chloe—"

"We made a promise to be honest with each other!" I continued, spewing more words out loud than I had in days. My voice cracked a few times from disuse, but I carried on, nonetheless. "Or does being the prince of Disgrace mean going back on your marriage vows? Have you no honor? I understand that I'm not very forthcoming right now, but *you* set a precedent. You are the one who—"

"Fine," he exclaimed, throwing his hands up in surrender and stalking away. I took a step to chase after him, only to realize that he was only moving away so that he could pace back and forth across the length of the bedroom. "You win, master debater."

I leaned against the post at the end of the bed and watched him rake his fingers through his tangled hair. It needed to be trimmed, and the light stubble forming on his jaw suggested that maintaining princely appearances had been the least of his concerns this past week.

"Whatever it is, you can tell me," I told him, softening my tone as he continued to pace with nervous energy. "If you're having an affair, then—"

Elijah froze, staring at me with wide eyes.

"You think I'm having an affair?" he whispered, the agitation melting out of his expression instantly. Before I knew it, he was rushing forward and taking my hands in his. "I'm not. Oh, gods, Chloe, I wouldn't— I'm so sorry that you would even think…"

It was my turn to freeze. His sudden proximity was alarming. Despite his frazzled, exhausted state, he was still as handsome as ever. I remembered the way my heart fluttered when he kissed my cheek at the altar, when he undid the laces of my wedding corset, and when he sat at my bedside and told me he thought I was beautiful.

I swallowed hard, pushing those distracting thoughts away.

"It's okay," I told him. "I didn't really think…"

When I trailed off, Elijah took the opportunity to speak again. "I'm just afraid that if I tell you the truth, you'll be upset with me. What I'm doing isn't technically wrong. My father knows, but he doesn't approve."

"What do you mean?" I pleaded. "Just tell me. I

won't be upset. If you tell me what you're doing, I'll tell you what I'm doing."

Elijah took a deep breath and squeezed my hands. They felt even smaller when they were engulfed by his, but I didn't mind. In spite of the tension in the air, his touch was undeniably comforting.

"I've been visiting the darkest pits of Hell," he admitted at last. "I've been going to see your sister. I didn't— I wasn't sure if you would disapprove. I mean, I know you girls aren't very fond of each other. It's just… I figured that, since I'm the prince of Disgrace, and she has been thoroughly disgraced, I could offer her some comfort."

In the silence that followed, I was aware of several things. I could hear the flames murmuring in the fireplace. Outside, an owl hooted in the night. Elijah held his breath, quiet as his eyes flickered across my face, waiting for my reaction. Elsewhere in the palace, my sisters and their princes slept. Beyond the Underworld, the endless realms of the universe spun like cogs and gears around their own spheres of existence.

All of those things were happening, but all I could focus on was the thudding of my heartbeat and the golden streaks of light in Elijah's eyes.

He was visiting my sister. Every day, he was descending into the darkest pits of Hell to see Rose. To comfort her. Because he thought it was the right thing for him to do. He did have honor. He was an honorable man. I tried to wrap my mind around it.

I was speechless. It was the last thing I expected to hear, though I truly didn't know what to imagine regarding his absence. At that moment, I could see the young prince for who he truly was. In spite of who his father was and where he was born, he was a good person with a good heart.

"Please say something," Elijah begged, his voice barely louder than a whisper.

But I couldn't. I didn't know what to say. For a girl who spent her days consuming words like they were sweet wine, I was at a loss. In the absence of my most dependable source of sustenance, all I had left were my bare instincts.

So, instead of saying anything at all, I chose action. I let go of Elijah's hands and lifted my own to his face. The uncertainty that trembled in his gaze told me he thought I was about to push him away, but then my fingertips brushed his jaw as my arms moved to wrap around his shoulders, and that doubt quickly turned to surprise.

And then, before he could settle on another

emotion, I reached up on the tips of my toes and kissed him.

Elijah's reaction was instantaneous. His hands wound around my waist, pulling me closer. I melted into him as his lips responded to mine with unexpected confidence.

That's when I decided that this wasn't Hell. It couldn't be. If Elijah was here and he could kiss me like this, it had to be heaven.

CHAPTER 10

"**A**re you sure you want to do this?" Elijah asked me, weaving his fingers through mine as I settled into the seat of the carriage beside him.

"No," I whispered. "Well, yes. But, also, no. I'm scared."

"I would be concerned if you weren't," he replied as the carriage set off. "It's not a pleasant place, to say the least."

I sighed and straightened my shoulders with determination.

"Rose has been down there for more than a month," I said. "I can handle a couple of hours. I'm just surprised that your father allowed it."

Elijah shrugged. "He doesn't see it as defiance.

But, if he catches on that you're in the process of attempting to defy him, I don't think he'll be quite so tolerant."

"Right. I'll be careful," I replied. "He doesn't know what we've asked the library, does he? You know, because he created it…"

"No, he can't," answered Elijah. I breathed a sigh of relief. "It's oddly sentient, but it's no more loyal to him than it is to anyone else who uses it. Actually, I have a theory that the library has been growing more emotionally intelligent over the centuries."

"Oh?"

"My father told me that I'm ridiculous for thinking so," Elijah continued with an eye roll. "He doesn't believe that anything he has created could dare to have a mind of its own, separate from his will."

The double meaning in his statement was obvious. The God of the Underworld didn't merely create the library, but so did the boy in front of me.

I squeezed his hand. "Well, if it's any consolation, I support your theory. I swear that place has a sarcastic streak."

Elijah chuckled. It was a few minutes after dawn. The entrance to the darkest pits of Hell wasn't far from the palace. Part of me wished the journey were longer so that I could have a chance to emotionally prepare myself a little better, but another part of me was glad that my mind wouldn't have a significant amount of time to torture me with dreadful anticipation.

I should've been more tired. The kiss that Elijah and I shared last night turned heated, escalating with blinding fervor until, before I knew it, he was hovering above me in the sheets of our bed, and both of us were gasping for breath. After that, we agreed it was best to cool things down and take it—whatever *it* was—slow.

So, then we talked.

I told him everything about my efforts to learn every single thing I could about divine laws in hopes of cutting Rose's sentence short. I shared my research with him. In turn, he told me about his visits with my sister. Apparently, she stayed silent for the most part, too exhausted by the overwhelming darkness of her prison to speak. When I asked him what Elijah did to comfort her, he told me that he spent most of the day reading to her.

That made me want to kiss him all over again, but I held myself back.

When I asked him if I could go with him, he was hesitant. Going to the darkest pits of Hell wasn't something that anyone did lightly. In fact, it wasn't something anyone did at all unless they were being sent there for punishment. There weren't even guards. There was no need for them. However, using my fledgling debate skills, I convinced him to take me with him. We dozed off after that, but the moment that the sun began to lighten, Elijah sought out his father and asked for his permission to bring me to the pits to see my sister.

The carriage pulled to a stop in front of an unmarked building constructed from black stones. It was the size of a cottage but without windows and nothing but a gaping black archway for a door. We'd gone in the opposite direction of the city that bustled at the foot of the God of the Underworld's palace and were instead in the middle of a quiet, foggy forest of spindly trees and soft grass.

Elijah helped me out of the carriage and led me to the building. My stomach dropped as we drew closer, and the carriage pulled away.

"You can probably feel your mood changing," Elijah murmured, holding my hand securely in his. "It's hard to feel optimistic down there. It sucks the joy out of you, but just remind yourself that it isn't permanent, and you'll feel normal again once you leave."

I nodded, then reached deep for courage. "Can I ask you something?"

We paused a few feet from the archway. I couldn't see beyond the shadows, though I swore I could hear an ominous chorus of whispers coming from within.

"Of course," Elijah murmured.

"How many people are down there?"

"As in, prisoners? Not many. A few hundred at most. You already know this, it's... a rare punishment."

I flinched. A few hundred tortured souls out of the billions of people in the universe, and my sister was one of them. If anything, that knowledge only strengthened my resolve.

"And Lilith is one of them?" I dared to ask.

Elijah stiffened at the mention of the demon. Lilith was ancient history, locked away before his father fell in love with his mother, Raya.

"Yes," he replied.

My next question was a risk, but I had to ask it.

"And have you ever seen a Lilith snake down there?"

He cursed under his breath and then stepped in front of me, holding my shoulders as he stood in between me and the archway.

"No, I haven't," he murmured, eyes large and bright with concern. "And you should pray that you don't, either. Listen to me, Chloe. You have to be careful about the things you say when we're down there. The darkest pits manifest our nightmares. If we give in to the darkness and allow it to feed on our fear, it won't hesitate to turn those fears into reality."

"I understand," I replied. "Nothing but rainbows and butterflies."

Every new thing I learned about the pits, every warning I received, made me feel more sad for Rose. It was inhumane to do this to someone like her.

Elijah leaned down and pressed a kiss to my forehead. When he pulled away, he offered me a small smile.

"Ready?" he asked me.

I nodded, clutching his hand tightly as we stepped to the very edge of the archway. As I was instructed earlier, I unwillingly pried my hand out of his and wrapped my arms around Elijah's waist.

"Hold on tightly to me," he murmured. "It's a long drop."

"I won't let go," I promised.

Without further ado, Elijah embraced me firmly,

clutching my body to his before throwing both of us through the pitch-black doorway.

There was no floor to land on. There was nothing.

The breath rushed out of my lungs as we plunged into pure darkness and fell through open space. Icy air whipped past us, ruffling my clothes and my hair. I buried my face in Elijah's chest, tightening my grip on him. As we fell, I expected silence, but there were a thousand terrifying sounds waiting for us in the dark. Sharp snaps, creaking groans, and pained howls echoed from all directions. I trembled, nearly letting out a cry when a disembodied, petrified scream sailed past my ear.

I was so afraid, but I couldn't be. I couldn't let the pits feed on my fear, as Elijah had said. Instead, I focused on him. I listened for the thrum of his heart inside his chest and breathed in the scent of him, allowing his warmth to soothe me into the closest thing to calm I could manage.

It could have been for minutes or for years that we fell, but eventually, our trajectory slowed, halting us mere inches from a gray stone floor before dropping us onto our feet. I stumbled in the sudden stillness. Elijah reached out to steady me.

The first thing I did was glance upwards, finding

nothing but a ceiling of squirming shadows, the hungry mouth of the awful thing that we'd just fallen through. I could still hear the frightening cries and spine-chilling moans.

We stood in a small, circular room. The walls and the floor were bare, smooth stone. No doors, no hallways, and certainly no windows.

Elijah guided me to the wall and pulled a glass vial of black liquid from inside his jacket. He tugged off the stopper and dipped the tip of his finger into the small container.

"My father's blood," he explained, painting a simple *X* on the wall. "It's the only way to get in and out, and it only works if he willingly gave it to you."

"Creepy."

"Tell me about it," Elijah sighed. As the dark, bloody *X* began to dry on the stone, Elijah wiped his finger off with a handkerchief and then slipped the vial back into his pocket. Calm focus fell over his face. He cleared his throat. "We are here as free visitors. We would like to see Rose the demigoddess, firstborn daughter of Zoren."

Something behind the wall groaned, low and threatening. I clutched onto Elijah's arm and huddled pathetically close; he was the only thing that reminded me of light as darkness clouded my veins, dragging me into an artificial melancholy. Before us, the wall began to crumble where he painted it with the God of the Underworld's blood. Within a minute, a jagged opening revealed a long hallway full of shadows, though I couldn't locate the source of light that they interrupted. In the distance was a plain black door.

Elijah glanced down at me.

"How are you feeling?" he asked.

"Awful," I replied truthfully. "But I want to keep going."

"This is the worst part," Elijah told me, gesturing to the hall before us. "Just walk fast and don't listen to anything they say."

I couldn't bring myself to ask him to elaborate, but I understood the second we took our first step into the hallway.

"Let me out of here!" screamed a woman's voice.

I gasped and spun around, but where there had once been a crumbled hole in the wall was smooth stone once more.

"Ignore them," Elijah reminded me, tugging me along beside him. I obeyed him, and we set off at a jog. However, no matter how fast we moved, we couldn't drown out the tortured cries of the prisoners, though they couldn't be seen.

"Please! Please, make it stop!"

"I'm begging... Please save me..."

"Prince Elijah, I'll do anything!"

"Show mercy, Princess Chloe..."

They knew our names. How did they know our names? How did they know we were here?

I picked up my pace into a run, and Elijah followed suit. With a rush of terror, I realized that the screams weren't of the prisoners but of something much darker beckoning to us from the shadows. Whatever it was, it wanted us to give in. It wanted us to answer, to stop, to be stuck here forever.

Finally, we threw ourselves against the door at the end of the hall, and Elijah twisted the knob with a low grunt. I tripped after him, practically falling into the next room before I managed to catch myself... on the velvet arm of a grand chaise lounge.

A plush green rug cushioned the soles of my shoes, and the pleasant scent of fresh cotton and wildflowers floated into my nose with my next inhale. When I straightened up, I found myself in a beautifully decorated room. The doorway behind me melted into ivory wallpaper adorned with delicate blue flowers. Golden sunshine streamed in through a pair of French windows on the opposite wall, revealing a lush meadow beyond. Gossamer curtains billowed in the warm breeze that filled the room with summer sweetness.

I looked to Elijah for answers, but he was watching me take in the scene with unease.

None of it made sense. We were supposed to be in the darkest pits of Hell. Why did it look like we had stumbled into a charming country cottage? My eyes swept the small space, noticing a cheerful kitchenette in the corner, a pretty vanity against the wall, and a cloud-like bed laden with a duvet and pillows woven from delicate eyelet lace.

There was a harp, too. It glimmered in the sunlight, the frame crafted from smooth glass and the strings sparkling as though woven from pure silver.

"I don't understand," I breathed.

Elijah placed his hand on the small of my back, rubbing the pad of his thumb in small circles.

"It's a representation of Rose's ideal life," Elijah explained, "More than anything, she craves simplicity, solitude, and sunlight. She wants to be free."

Applying gentle pressure with his hand, Elijah guided me to the bed.

"It one of the many tortures of the darkest pits of Hell," he continued. "Because the prisoner does not have the strength to enjoy what they desire the most. Other tortures come into play when the perfect scene before them is twisted with their fears, but I won't get into that..."

That's when I saw Rose. Small, frail, and so pale that she blended in with the bedding at first, she lay under the covers and stared at the ceiling with a blank expression. My knees trembled as I took in the sight of her. She looked like a shell of her former self, and her haggard appearance was made worse by the beautiful surroundings. Her cheeks were sallow, her skin had taken on a grayish pallor, and her lips were purplish-blue.

If not for the shallow rise and fall of her chest, I would think I was looking at my sister's corpse. She was so thin, so colorless... it was a far cry from the stunning woman with light-brown hair and glittering eyes that used to sit next to me at our father's dinner table. Rose always had a pretty rosiness in her cheeks, a perpetual blush that endeared her to others and paired well with her graceful humility. That was gone now.

"Hi, Rose," Elijah murmured, sitting down on the edge of the bed and offering her a smile as she turned her head slowly, as if it required Herculean effort, in our direction. "I'm back. I brought someone with me this time."

Something akin to surprise passed like a ghost in Rose's gaze as she met my eyes. I smiled, standing at the edge of the bed, overcome with emotion and trying to choke it down. I didn't want her to see me cry. It didn't seem fair to force her to witness that. After all, what did I have to cry about? I wasn't the prisoner.

"Hello," I said to her. "I hope it's okay that I came to see you."

"Chloe," she murmured, her voice hoarse and shaky.

Elijah patted the mattress in front of him, motioning for me to take a seat.

"Being close to people from above helps her regain a little bit of strength," he told me. Without hesitation, I climbed on top of the covers and tucked my legs underneath me.

Rose swallowed, her thin neck twitching with the effort.

"You are so pretty, Chloe… like I remember…" she breathed. "Are you going to kill me, too?"

CHAPTER 11

Overcome with shock at Rose's question, I glanced at Elijah.

He cringed and then reached out to pat Rose's bony shoulder, which was clothed in a soft, butter-yellow fabric.

"It's okay, Rose," he murmured. "She's real. She's not here to hurt you. Do you want me to help you sit up?"

Rose gave him an almost imperceptible nod. Thus began the painful-to-witness process of her struggling to lift herself from the pillows. Elijah did most of the work, hooking his hands under her arms to hoist her up like a doll and prop her up against the headboard. When he was finished, Rose sat there limply, her hands resting weakly in her lap.

She looked at me again with her hollow, black eyes.

"I see our sister sometimes," she rasped. "She crawls into bed beside me like a child—"

Rose's entire body heaved with a horrifying cough, forcing her to pause her story.

"—and then she takes out a knife and stabs me in the heart."

I didn't need to ask which sister it was that Rose imagined murdering her. A chill ran down my spine. However, what Elijah said did seem to be true. With both of us in the bed with her, she appeared to be regaining the barest hint of color.

Even if I wasn't petrified, I wouldn't know what to say to her. In our father's kingdom, Rose and I did not speak much. We kept to ourselves. She played her music, and I read my books.

For a second, I considered telling her that Riven wasn't doing so well out there above the darkest pits, but then I remembered the way Elijah reacted when I mentioned Lilith snakes before. I hadn't even told him yet what I discovered about Riven. Plus, I didn't think it would bring Rose much satisfaction to know that her twin was suffering, too. She wasn't malicious or vengeful like that.

"Is there something I can do to make you more

comfortable?" I asked her, feeling utterly useless. "I can try to play the harp—"

"The prince comes, too," Rose murmured, ignoring my offer. It was probably for the best. I had read into music theory before, but I wasn't gifted at playing instruments like she was.

"The prince?" I replied, glancing at Elijah. He frowned and shook his head. It seemed he'd heard these things before, perhaps explained to him when he first visited Rose.

"Finn," she croaked. "When I am sleeping, he wakes me and calls me cruel names, then smothers me with a pillow. Every time I die, I come back. It is exhausting."

"Rose," I whispered, scooting closer to her. I grabbed her hand, trying not to recoil at how cold and rough her skin was.

"Our father, too," she added, eyelids fluttering with the effort it took to list out the names of the hallucinations who came to torture her. "Gia... she breaks my harp and cuts my throat with the shards of glass... and Evangeline... she sets the cottage on fire..."

I didn't know who Evangeline was but asking would only bring her more pain. Even though I knew my efforts were futile, I tried to rub some warmth into her hands.

"It's okay, Rose," I told her. "It will be over soon, I promise. I'm going to find a way to get you out of here. I know we haven't been very close sisters, but I know you don't deserve this kind of punishment. I won't stop until you're free from this prison. You can trust me."

Rose blinked. She had no reaction to my bold declarations, or perhaps she simply didn't have the energy to emote. Elijah remained still and quiet beside her, glancing between the two of us with kind, patient eyes.

My sister coughed again. Her thumb and index finger twitched in my hand, and I wondered if that was her attempt at tightening her grip on me.

"I never see him," she mumbled. "Asher. He never comes."

"I'm so sorry, Rose," I replied, flinching at the memory of the rope pulling taut as Asher was hung in front of everyone. I didn't have the strength to watch the golden-haired boy die, but I'd heard every second of it. "I know you loved him."

She let out an exhale that was slightly louder than the one before it—the best version of a sigh she could manage in her current state.

"I barely knew him," she corrected me. "Yet he made me happy. He was the only thing… the only light in that place. He was my friend. Asher was kind to me like no one else…"

Rose shivered.

Confusion kept me from holding my tongue.

"I don't understand," I murmured. "I thought you two…"

Her gaze drifted from mine, settling on a distant point across the room.

"We shared a kiss. That is all," she said. "I wanted the chance to fall in love with him. I couldn't… the prince… Asher helped me escape, and I asked him to come with me. I didn't want to be alone. That is what I deserve to be punished for. It is my fault he is dead."

My sister's eyelids drifted shut. A single tear fell from the corner of one eye, trailing down her ghostly cheek. As her story sunk in, I felt my throat get tight, but I fought the urge to cry. When I looked at Elijah, I could tell it was his first time hearing Rose speak of the mortal boy.

Nobody knew the truth.

They thought Rose was an adulteress. They believed she cheated on Prince Finn throughout their engagement and then ran away with her lover on her wedding day to purposefully drive home the point that she never wanted the prince. They imagined her a reckless woman, spitting in the face of the God of the Underworld and her own father, throwing away duty in favor of an affair with a servant. None of it ever sounded quite right to me, but I had no evidence to assume anything else.

Those who thought ill of Rose couldn't be more wrong. Anyone who came to see her like this would know that she was so scared. She feared everyone. Our father, the God of the Underworld, Prince Finn... She was doomed to darkness, and all she wanted was to live in the light. Asher gave her hope, so she latched on to him because he was the only thing keeping her together.

What I didn't understand was why Rose didn't try to defend herself. Why didn't she try to explain the truth to the God of the Underworld when she and Asher were captured?

The answer came to me seconds later with disturbing clarity.

It would've been useless for her to argue her case. As long as nobody else knew the truth, the God of the Underworld didn't care what her true reasons for running away were. The point was that she embarrassed him, dared to defy him, and betrayed his eldest son. A god with injured pride cared little for the rebuttals of a twenty-one-year-old demigoddess. Rose understood that above all else, it seemed, so she let the god believe what he wanted to and accepted her fate.

We were always at their mercy, those almighty gods. We were not in control of our pasts, presents, or futures, even if we fooled ourselves into thinking otherwise. The gods would always seek to serve themselves before anyone else.

The silence stretched on for ages, settling heavily on the horribly lovely room. Rose kept her eyes closed, but somehow I knew that she wasn't asleep. I held her hand and glared at the duvet, angry and sad and terrified and disgusted all at once.

Eventually, Elijah broke the silence.

"I brought a new book today," he said, tugging a small novel from his jacket and showing it to Rose as she slowly opened her eyes.

I leaned over to see the cover. It was *A Little Prince* by Antoine de Saint-Exupéry. Although it was a children's book written by a mortal man many decades ago, it was one of my favorite stories. It was sad but in a beautiful way. I smiled at Elijah.

"You brought that copy from the Disgrace library," I murmured. "I recognize it."

"I asked Zak to fetch it for me before he came to my father's palace," he replied, then glanced at Rose. "Shall I read it?"

Rose's eyes slid from me to Elijah slowly. Then, so delicately that I wondered if it was a trick of the light, the corners of her mouth lifted in a weak smile.

"Yes," she breathed. "Please."

When we returned to the palace, I felt the darkest pits of Hell lingering on me as if I had brought some of it home with me. It tugged on my frayed nerves and tried to unravel my hopeful heart. I sat down by the fire in the bedroom and took deep, steadying breaths. The pleading screams and tortured moans echoed in the back of my mind.

Elijah knelt beside me and draped a blanket around my shoulders, keeping his arms around me. His presence helped me feel less terrified, and I couldn't help thinking about how ironic it was that a prince of Hell would have such a healing aura.

"You handled that remarkably well," Elijah murmured.

I stared into the flames of the hearth and huffed a

humorless breath of laughter. "I'm huddled on the floor like a child."

"Many men who might claim to be mightier than you have crumbled apart after visiting the darkest pits," he replied. I thought of the story of Maurice, but he was imprisoned down there for a century. I was there for a day, and already I could understand why he would end his own life to escape the cold that leeched into my bones and refused to let go.

I shivered. "It's an awful place. She shouldn't be down there. How can your father…?"

I trailed off, remembering that I was in the God of the Underworld's palace. Speaking against him was not a good idea.

"I know," Elijah whispered. It was the only way he could tell me that he agreed his father's punishment against Rose was too harsh.

For the next few minutes, I slowly thawed in his embrace, just enough to wriggle out of the blanket and stretch out on the carpet, staring up at the ceiling. With a sigh, Elijah lay down beside me, leaving several inches of space as if he was suddenly afraid of smothering me.

"I need to tell you something," I murmured, keeping my gaze trained on the high ceiling above us.

"I'm listening."

"It's just… I want you to know the reason I asked about the Lilith snakes," I said, unable to turn my head to see if he flinched again at the mention of the dark creatures. "I think there's something going on with Riven…"

I told him about my sister, laying out the evidence that she was being haunted by a Lilith snake. I described what I saw at Rose's trial and then what I witnessed on the balcony the night of our wedding. He listened so patiently that I even felt brave enough to admit that I was struggling to feel bad for Riven.

"I understand," Elijah responded to my guilty admittance. "I know that your sister is rather cold, but perhaps she has reasonable motivations? Surely she doesn't deserve to be led to her doom."

I frowned. "Maybe she doesn't necessarily deserve it, but I also don't feel inclined to help her."

"Well, perhaps we should just keep an eye on her for now," he suggested lightly. "The Lilith snakes work in mysterious and convoluted ways, and I would hate for you to get caught in any unexpected crosshairs. They are, after all, working for a demon."

"Please don't think I'm crazy for asking this, but

is it possible to visit her? The same way we visited Rose?"

Lips parted in horror, Elijah sat up. "Chloe—"

"No! I don't *want* to," I said quickly, sitting up and waving my hands in denial. "I just meant… isn't it a really bad thing that a terrifying demon could be that accessible? If the wrong person got their hands on the vial of blood your father gave you, it could be disastrous."

Elijah shook his head. "Actually, she is the only prisoner who cannot be visited. It is part of the curse on the place. If anyone goes down there with the intention to seek out Lilith, they will be imprisoned for eternity alongside her. Hence why I just reacted the way I did when you asked that question."

"Right," I muttered sheepishly. "Sorry."

"Much to my father's annoyance, there are quite a few people down there who are imprisoned for that very reason," he told me, settled back down on the floor with his head propped up on his elbow. "The demon had many loyal followers. In fact…"

"What?"

"It's just that there's a theory…"

"Go on," I urged him, hugging my knees to my chest.

A crease formed between Elijah's eyebrows as an

anxious expression took over his face. "Well, I have a suspicion that my father doesn't truly know the extent of what goes on down there."

"How is that possible? He's the one who made the prison."

"When we were younger, he described the pits to my brothers and me with terrible but vague details. We never had any reason to go down there ourselves, so we never questioned it. Not that anyone would question father," Elijah murmured. "The first time I went down there was last week and, when I saw what your sister was enduring, I realized that my father never mentioned any of it. His explanation got me as far as the blood marking on the wall, and then I had to figure out the rest by myself. When I walked down that hallway for the first time…"

Elijah shivered.

"He didn't warn you at all?" I gasped.

"I don't think he knew," he said, leaning in and lowering his voice. "Your sister's beautiful prison cell isn't really his style of torture."

"I'm confused."

"Well, that's where the theory comes in," he continued. "Some say that the God of the Underworld is not the only architect of the darkest pits of

Hell. In fact, there are some scholars who posit that, yes, the God of the Underworld created the pits to be Lilith's prison, but that he relinquished control the moment she was locked inside. He threw away the key and walked away for thousands of years. Only in recent centuries has he started tossing prisoners inside with her."

"Are you suggesting that Lilith is the one in control of that place?"

"Think about it," Elijah said. "Demons have the power to uncover your deepest desires, don't they?"

"I suppose."

"And Rose's prison cell was a flawless translation of what she desires most in the world, right?"

I swallowed down my fear as cold dread crawled down my spine like frost.

"Right."

"*And* you remember what the prison cells in the pits of Disgrace looked like, don't you? The ones that are definitely designed by my father?"

I cringed at the memory of the tour I took when I first arrived in Disgrace, a formal duty that was required of all of us. After all, how could we be proper princesses of the kingdoms if we did not see the prisoners caged in our respective section of the Underworld for ourselves?

Down there, the cells that trapped sinful mortal souls for eternity were barren, dirty rooms with iron bars. The God of the Underworld was very literal with his intentions. He imprisoned the dead, and, thus, it would look exactly like a prison. The god certainly wouldn't bother giving them a lush, green meadow or a wonderful feather bed.

"So the God of the Underworld doesn't even know that he's subjecting people to his ex-wife's personal torture playground when he banishes them to the darkest pits?" I breathed. "He doesn't know he's… feeding her?"

"No, I don't think so," Elijah replied. "I'm trying to figure out the right way to tell him."

As it turned out, Riven wasn't the only sister of mine who was at the mercy of an ancient demon.

"This is all so complicated," I moaned.

"There's something else, too," he muttered. "I think Nico is up to something?"

I didn't expect him to bring up his brother so casually, but we had spent the entire day talking about my sister, so it was only fair.

"Like what?" I inquired.

"I don't know," Elijah grumbled, glaring at the ceiling as if merely thinking about Nico made him frustrated. "I'm not the only one leaving the palace. I think he's going back to Corruption, but I haven't had the chance to figure out what for. With the way he's been acting ever since Riven and Finn were married, I can't help thinking that he might be dangerously vengeful. Nico has a temper."

"Maybe you could follow him?"

"No, that wouldn't work. He would know it was me. My brothers have learned to be on guard from each other with divine precision. But I need to find a way to keep an eye on him, just like Riven."

I bit my lip. "Well…"

"…what?"

I had an idea brewing in the back of my mind, but I wasn't sure if Elijah would receive it well. It was worth a shot.

"Since I can't go down into the darkest pits by myself, it's best if you're the one who keeps the task of visiting Rose whenever you can," I began. "And while you're helping my sister stay as sane as possible while we look for a solution, I can repay you by following your brother and figuring out if he's up to anything."

"I hate the sound of that."

"I knew you would."

"Chloe… Nico isn't like me. He's not even like Finn," he sighed. "There's something a little unstable about him. I mean, I guess he's *corrupted*. Duh. He's unpredictable and dangerous."

"But I am incredibly methodical, intelligent, and I have a literal god for a husband," I countered. "So, aren't I well-equipped for the task?"

Elijah ran his hands through his hair. It was late, and we were both tired, but neither one of us could stand the idea of wasting time sleeping when there was so much to be done.

Unfair imprisonment, demonic snakes, and vengeful princes… something dark was brewing in the Underworld.

Darker than normal, that is.

"I really don't want you to do this."

"I know."

"Chloe…"

"I'll be fine," I told Elijah, reaching up to press a kiss to his cheek to emphasize my point. "There comes a time in every scholar's life where they must do fieldwork in order to improve their research, right?"

Elijah frowned down at me. "Following my brother to who-knows-where in Hell is hardly fieldwork."

I fixed him with a firm stare. "We agreed that this would be my role, Elijah."

He let out a low sigh, drawing it out for several seconds until he finally nodded and produced a thin silver chain from his pocket. Unlike his brothers, who focused their divine powers on dominance and strength, Elijah was studying the art of charms and enchantments. Gods and goddesses had many gifts; curses and blessings were among the more commonly known ones.

Elijah told me that he wasn't interested in learning how to curse others, but he was working on ways to embed items with blessings for protection.

"I have a grand plan, you see," he whispered to me the night before when we finally crawled into bed, his eyes bright with excitement. "I want to find a way to prevent mortals from being unfairly pulled into the Underworld when they die. Sometimes, the disgraced or the corrupt or the arrogant—or whatever—have committed small crimes, but my father snatches them up to feed his realm. But, if I can charm these little trinkets with protections and positive blessings, maybe I can help a few people in the mortal realm turn their lives around. And they won't even know that a god is intervening on their behalf!"

It was an ambitious goal, one that would take centuries for Elijah to gain the strength and ability to accomplish—and one that would enrage his father if he found out. However, it spoke to Elijah's unfailingly good heart.

I was falling deeply for him. There was no more denying it. He was so much more than I ever could have dreamed of in a husband. Maybe a god had sent *me* a blessing without my realizing it.

In the reception room of our private chambers, Elijah wrapped the silver chain around my wrist three times and then fastened it securely. The second he let go, he gasped and then broke into a smile. When I glanced down, my body was gone.

I was invisible.

"You did it!" I exclaimed. "You actually did it!"

Then, forgetting that Elijah could no longer see me, I threw my arms around him. He awkwardly responded to the embrace, draping his arms around where he thought my shoulders were.

"This is so weird," he chuckled. "But so cool."

Stepping back, I grinned at him. He stared at the empty space just slightly to my right, causing me to reach out with my hands and guide his face to the side that he was facing me properly.

"Okay," I told him. "I'm ready."

"Just remember that, even though the bracelet makes you invisible, you can still be heard," Elijah told me. "Also, the charm itself probably won't hold up against an older or more powerful god, so just try to stay hidden no matter what."

"Got it."

"And I'm off to the darkest pits. I'll give Rose your regards."

"Thank you," I whispered.

Together, we slipped out of our private rooms and parted ways. While Elijah went down to catch his carriage to the haunting entrance to the pits, I went to Nico's private chambers. My plan was to stake out his door and wait for him to emerge so that I could follow him.

Secretly, I hoped that Elijah was just being paranoid about his older brother, but I trusted his concern. Best case scenario, I was about to find out that Nico was leaving the palace to meditate in the forest, and he wasn't up to anything suspicious.

Worst case scenario… Well, I'd cross that bridge when I came to it.

As I hurried down the halls, servants walked past me without curtsying or bowing, proving that Elijah's invisibility blessing was working perfectly. However, I noticed a few of them glance over their shoulders in confusion when I passed by. That's when I noticed the sound of my footsteps echoing on the marble and immediately lightened my tread.

When I rounded the corner to the hall where Nico's rooms were located—not far from Prince

Finn and Riven, I realized with a cringe—I discovered that I was right on time. Just as his door came into view, it cracked open, and Nico emerged from within. At once, he started down the hall toward me at a brisk pace, his expression stormy and thin-lipped. I froze, holding my breath and pressing myself to the wall as Nico's eyes trailed over the spot where I was standing.

He didn't see me.

The charm was working perfectly. I couldn't wait to tell Elijah.

I had to jog to keep up with Nico as he wove downstairs toward the back of the palace. He seemed distracted, muttering under his breath as he stomped along. Servants stumbled into respectful bows as he stormed past them, but he didn't spare any of them a glance. Thankfully, his lack of focus on his surroundings meant that I could get away with the sound of rustling fabric that my clothing made as I scurried along behind him at a safe distance. I was wearing trousers and a snug, long-sleeved sweater that day instead of a princess-appropriate dress; Elijah and I both agreed that the outfit would make it easier for me to move around undetected during the day's mission.

We passed no one of importance on our way to

the rear entrance of the palace, the one that opened up to the gardens and the forest beyond. Nico and Elijah were the only princes awake at this hour, apparently.

The gardens presented more of a challenge once Nico burst through the doors and stomped down the gravel path. I had to get uncomfortably close to him in order to pass through the door before it shut again and then match my footsteps up to his so that the sound of my shoes crunching in the gravel didn't alert him to my presence.

My heart beat fast and heavy. Every so often, I glanced down to make sure the bracelet was still securely in place, terrified of what would happen if it fell off and I was left utterly exposed. I didn't have a weapon, not that it would do any use against a god… and I wasn't quite sure what kind of excuse I could offer for my behavior if Nico caught me.

Hopefully, if the worst happened, I could come up with something in the moment.

Nico stepped off the gravel path and traipsed through the grass to the black wisteria archway that led to the banks of the Red River. I felt a trickle of hesitation but hurried after him. Was he visiting his mother? Was that it?

But the prince didn't stop by the water's edge to

call for Raya in the trickling, burgundy waters. He marched along the river, face turned toward the ground. I wished I could see his expression or hear what he was saying to himself, but I didn't dare get closer than a couple of yards.

Eventually, a narrow dirt path presented itself at the edge of the forest. Swallowing back my fear, I followed him into the trees. A layer of fog crept across the ground, clinging to the tree roots that burst up through the grass and making the hems of my trousers slightly damp. The sun was only just starting to turn the sky pastel yellow, the grayness of night holding on tightly to the horizon, but I had a feeling that the fog wouldn't burn off even when the sun rose high into the sky. The forest had an eerie quality to it; the perpetual fog was likely the least disturbing thing I might run across within its shadowy brush.

Thankfully, Nico didn't go far into the forest. Rather, he followed the path to a small clearing, where a carriage was waiting for him. Painted silver and black, it was obvious that the carriage had come from the kingdom of Corruption.

Nico glanced over his shoulder before flinging open the door to the carriage and climbing inside, jostling the horse and driver wordlessly. My stomach twisted. I prayed that I wouldn't have to follow him too far that morning, and Elijah insisted that I should back out the second that I was uncomfortable, but I was determined to pull my weight. If Elijah was kind enough to descend into the darkest pits yet again to comfort my sister, I could be brave enough to find out what kind of threat, if any, Nico's vengeful spirit posed to all of us.

I had to act quick. The groan of the carriage wheels and the clanking of the horse's royal attire covered the sound of me running toward the carriage as it pulled away and throwing myself onto the back ledge where luggage was usually stored. I held onto the low railing that skirted the perimeter of the ledge for dear life as the carriage took off down a narrow forest lane. If the driver noticed any unexpected weight clinging on, he didn't stop to inspect the carriage. He'd probably learned not to ask questions where Prince Nico was concerned.

I huddled in the back as the carriage swayed precariously on the bumpy road, trying not to let out any squeaks of gasps of anxiety as the possibility of me falling out and being abandoned in the middle of the woods sat ever-present in the forefront of my mind.

Luckily, the kingdom of Corruption wasn't far

from the palace of the God of the Underworld. Just as with Arrogance, the King of Hell kept his oldest sons close. I was grateful for it at that moment. If Corruption was as far away as Disgrace, I would be forced to hold on for dear life for hours. Instead, I only had to endure for half an hour before we pulled up in front of a looming palace.

I barely had time to observe the exterior of the palace of Corruption before Nico threw open the door of the carriage and stormed inside his home, but what I did see was very different than what I was used to in Disgrace. Nico's palace was constructed of black stone, all jagged edges and nightmarish spikes of turrets and towers stabbing the sky above. It looked more like an evil lair than a prince's palace.

Inside, it was just as spooky.

For a second, I found myself thinking that it was no wonder Riven manipulated her way into a different marriage. I couldn't imagine Prince Finn's palace in Arrogance was as simultaneously gaudy and disturbing as this. Every inch of the palace's interior told me that Nico was desperately trying to prove himself. I didn't necessarily want to psychoanalyze him, but I imagined it was easy for the second son to develop an inferiority complex.

Maybe that's why Riven was the way that she

was. She'd been born only minutes after Rose, after all. She was so close to being the firstborn—and that was clearly what she'd wanted all along. Was Nico the same? Was that something they'd bonded over during their brief engagement?

Corruption was empty. Either the nobles who were left behind were late risers, or they'd left for their own estates until their prince was permitted to return from his father's home next year. We didn't pass a single servant as we wove through the black marble halls, though I imagined there had to be *someone* staying behind in his absence, right? Someone to dust away the cobwebs, surely?

It was difficult to keep up with Nico and even more difficult to hide my heavy breathing from the physical exertion of moving as fast as possible while making no noise. Nico remained lost in his thoughts, having no reason to suspect that someone had dared to stalk him all the way to Corruption.

I wouldn't allow myself to pause and think about all of the things that could go wrong if I made one wrong move.

We ended up in the throne room, which was adorned in silver. An austere chandelier hung from the ceiling, unlit and full of shadows as Nico moved down the long carpet and ducked behind the twin thrones resting on a dais at the head of the room. With a jolt, I thought about how Nico once believed Riven would sit on one of those thrones alongside him.

She was so cruel and yet still betrayed signs of having a conscience. Maybe Elijah was right when he suggested that Riven had a legitimate motivation for her heartless actions. If I made it out of my current situation unscathed, I could consider adding that to my list of things to research.

Behind the throne room was a private meeting room, as was the architectural custom of most palaces. When I carefully snuck through the crack in the doorway behind Nico, I expected to see a large table with plenty of chairs or perhaps a collection of comfortable sofas and armchairs.

Instead, I discovered that the room was completely bare except for an altar at the far end. The thick velvet curtains were drawn, the only source of light being two white-flame sconces on either side of the narrow chamber.

I hovered by the door, an overwhelming sense of *wrong* swimming in the pit of my stomach.

Nico walked to the altar and waved his hands, lighting dozens of candles all at once. When the flames illuminated the contents of the altar, I had to quietly clap my hands over my mouth to keep myself from making an audible exclamation of horror.

Atop the altar were three small mounds from which a dark substance dripped. When I dared to take a step closer, my head spun with fear as I realized the items were human hearts. Though obviously not freshly stolen, blood oozed from them as if fed by an unseen source.

Nausea gripped me, and I stumbled slightly. Still, Nico didn't sense my movement or betray any suspicion that there was somebody else in the room with him. He knelt at the base of the altar and lowered his head as if about to pray. Stealing myself, I tried not to look at the hearts—were they still *beating*?—and instead attempted to get a better look at Nico's face.

His eyes were closed, his veiny hands clenched tightly in his lap.

"Tell me what else I must do," he whispered. "I am ready for the next step."

Suddenly, Nico stiffened. He tilted his head to the side slightly as if listening to a voice I couldn't hear. Goosebumps erupted on my arms. He looked pale and utterly exhausted up close, dark shadows underneath his shut eyes.

"I'm willing to do whatever it takes," he murmured.

I glanced around, searching for his conversation partner, but I had a sickening feeling I knew exactly why I couldn't see or hear whom he was speaking to…

"No!" he suddenly shouted, eyes flying open. I flinched and took a step back, leaning against the wall and observing at Nico glared at the hearts on the altar. "She must not be harmed. You know that I do not blame her."

Whom was he talking about?

Nico's gaze took on a faraway quality, lips parted slightly in barely concealed fear as he listened to whatever his companion replied. I couldn't help thinking that he looked eerily similar to the way Riven appeared on the balcony that night.

But it couldn't be. Lilith snakes were terrifyingly monstrous, but they wouldn't dare to go after a prince of Hell, would they?

Then again, why wouldn't the serpentine servants of the God of the Underworld's ex-wife want to lead his sons to their doom?

Things were far more complicated and frightening than I expected. This was the worst-case scenario I feared when I left my chambers that morning. Nico was not innocently going for daily jaunts to clear his head, as I hoped, but returning to a bleeding altar at dawn to pray to a demon.

I wished I knew what he was asking for help with. I was too afraid to acknowledge the theories that were beginning to form in the furthest reaches of my mind.

"You keep telling me to be patient," Nico hissed. He sounded furious, his tone laced with poisonous wrath.

Just as I thought about how badly I wanted to suddenly be far, far away from this room, I looked down just in time to see a large, disembodied hand appear from the shadows and wrap tightly around my forearm. Just as a scream of horror began to form in my throat, the hand pulled me away from Nico.

All at once, I was no longer in the palace of Corruption but soaring through a smoky blue fog that smelled inexplicably of parchment. Then, before I could observe my gloomy kidnapper for a moment longer, I landed in a heap on the ornate carpet in front of the hearth in the reception room of my chambers in the palace of the God of the Underworld.

I was right back where I started that morning.

CHAPTER 13

"I did not expect you to be the type to go looking for trouble, Chloe."

It was difficult to get my bearings as I braced myself on my hands and knees on the floor of my room. Seconds before, I was standing in a dark room watching Nico speak to a being that I couldn't see or hear.

A Lilith snake.

Was there more than one? Had a second Lilith snake slithered up from the darkest pits of hell? Or was it the same one that was stalking Riven?

And, if so, why had it chosen to make targets out of those two specifically?

Questions spun on an endless loop in my mind, but it was nothing compared to the confusion I felt as I glanced down at my wrist and saw that the silver bracelet that Elijah blessed was broken, laying tangled and useless on the carpet. I stood up quickly to face the person who yanked me out of Corruption, though the sound of his voice was enough to confirm who it was before I laid eyes on them.

Zoren.

My father was perched on the edge of the tea table, dressed in wool trousers, a collared shirt, and matching vest. His salt-and-pepper hair was neatly combed, betraying nothing of the dizzying teleportation journey he just forced me to embark on with him. He wore spectacles with thin black frames, despite the fact that he was an immortal being with perfect eyesight. I always thought it was silly of him to wear the glasses, a pseudo-intellectual choice designed to make others unconsciously believe that they were less intelligent than him.

I hadn't seen my father since my and Elijah's wedding. Even then, I avoided him the best I could. We didn't have the best relationship, to say the least.

"How did you know I was there?" I asked him. The air tingled with the divine electricity that accompanied the presence of a god his age, placing unnatural pressure on my shoulders, but I refused to bow or show deference.

Suddenly, I was angrier than I'd felt in my entire life. It was an uncommon emotion for me; it felt like my spine was on fire. My mouth tasted oddly metallic. My hands were clenched into fists at my sides, trembling with the effort it took to conceal the overwhelming and sudden emotion.

In contrast, my father appeared infuriatingly calm.

"I followed you, of course," he replied. "I must say, the young prince's blessed object was very impressive, but there is much room for improvement. You are lucky that the infantile god of Corruption is both naive and distracted."

So, Nico couldn't see me, but my father could. It was a good thing I didn't run into the God of the Underworld during my thwarted mission, although it also wasn't ideal that I ran into my father.

"You were following me? Or you were following the prince and happened to see me in the process?" I asked, crossing my arms against my chest.

Zoren seemed amused by my standoffishness.

"My children have changed so much these past few months," he mused, observing me with wise eyes.

Admittedly, I was shocked. After our father announced that we'd been promised off to the six princes of the Underworld against our will, he dropped us off at the feet of the King of Hell and never spoke to us again. I did not see him again until Rose's trial, and then only a second and third time when he took his place in the pews at Riven's wedding, then mine.

I expected no less. When I was a child, my father wasn't particularly affectionate. Like most gods, he saw his children as a reflection of his power, so he only showed us favor when we impressed him enough to deserve it. He fostered a competitive spirit among my sisters and me, the goal being to push us to supersede each other and become even greater in the process.

From a young age, I never bought into it. I could see right through my father. I could see how proud and shallow he was, how everything he did was a performance with no true power behind it. He was a minor god at the end of the day, foolish enough to get tricked by the goddess of deceit and lose his entire kingdom.

That's how we were all here in the first place. Proving how little he cared for us, my father auctioned off his daughters to the God of the Underworld in exchange for his help in regaining his kingdom. So far, the allied gods had no luck.

"Have we changed?" I hissed at my father. "Or did you never truly know us in the first place?"

Zoren huffed out a breath of laughter. "How can you say that when I have just saved you from getting yourself involved in something dark and irreversible. I know how curious you are, Chloe. If I did not pull you from that cursed room, you wouldn't have made it out of there alive."

A chill ran down my spine, but it didn't quell my fury.

"What makes you so sure of that?" I snapped. "It is not wise to underestimate others, father."

He pursed his lips at me and then sighed loudly. "My daughters… You are all so beautiful. So multi-talented. Riven with her dancing and Amalia with her writing. Even that foolish firstborn of mine was a wonderful musician."

The way Zoren spoke of Rose in the past tense made me bristle, but he wasn't finished with his speech.

"And you," he continued, forming a deep frown as he trailed his eyes up and down my masculine attire. "What do you offer? Intellect? Knowledge? That is not my domain. Sometimes I wonder if you are truly my daughter at all, but it is no matter. Your mother always was a bit odd. You must have inherited some of that from her."

It took every ounce of willpower within me not to grab the nearest object, which happened to be a large vase filled with white peonies and throw it at my father's face. But I wasn't reckless. I could control my temper.

"Been thinking a lot about my mother, have you?" I spat.

It was cruel what he did to our mothers. He seduced them, impregnated them, and then brought them to the immortal realm to raise us. They were forced to leave their lives behind, but the moment that our marriages were secured, and they didn't serve a purpose, he banished them back to the mortal world. Their memories were stolen. Even if I sought out my mother one day, she wouldn't remember me. She wouldn't remember any of it.

"Not really," Zoren responded with a shrug. "Anyway, I only wanted to stop by and warn you not to get close to Prince Nico again. The second son is up to something."

Why Zoren was bothering to worry about Nico when he still didn't have a kingdom of his own was beyond me, but I figured he had a self-serving goal that he was keeping to himself.

I hated him. I hated my father. With so much evil surrounding me, I could only see *him* as the true villain.

I glared at him. "Yes, that seems to be a trend," I growled. "The second child behaving in wicked and mysterious ways."

Zoren narrowed his eyes. He knew I was referring to Riven, but his expression told me everything I needed to know about her calculating climb up to Prince Finn's throne. Our father was well aware of everything she was doing in that respect. Perhaps he was even the one who put her up to it, convincing her to betray Nico and take the newly available first-born the second that Rose was out of the picture.

And Riven, always stuck in Rose's shadow, leaped at the opportunity to prove that she was better suited for the role as the future Queen of Hell. Zoren knew she would. As he said, he understood us. He understood that Riven resented her twin for the few minutes of life she had over her, that Riven always believed that she had been cheated somehow.

"Don't look at me like that," Zoren scoffed. "What else was I supposed to do when that girl ran off with the servant?"

That girl.

"Say her name," I hissed.

"Excuse me?"

"Say her name, Father," I repeated, taking a step toward him. "She's your daughter. You created her. Why is it so hard for you to speak her name? Are you ashamed of her? Or are you too weak to acknowledge that it was your fault she ran away in the first place?"

The furniture trembled with the rage that poured off my father, but I didn't shy away from him. I'd never spoken to him this way, but it felt good to stand up to him. I didn't realize how many negative feelings toward him I'd bottled up over the years. Now it felt impossible to keep them inside; I feared I was about to explode.

"Watch your tongue," Zoren rumbled, deep and godly.

I'd gone too far with my accusations, but there wasn't an ounce of regret inside me. I wanted him to know that I hated him, that none of his daughters truly respected him. He thought he was mighty because he treated us like pawns, but even the God of the Underworld, who was far more powerful than him, didn't treat his sons this way.

My anger knew no limits. As I glared at my father, all I could think about was Rose, down in her horrible prison, hallucinating a thousand deaths at the hands of the people she feared most, surrounded by beauty that she could not enjoy. At the root of her tragedy, it was our father's fault she was down there.

"That girl made her choice," argued Zoren when I didn't respond right away. "What else should I have done besides disown her?"

I threw my arms up in exasperation. "You should have loved her! You should have been a father to her. You should have *protected* her. You should have understood that she was afraid, and she wanted a different life than the one you designed for her."

"I did my best—"

"No!" I shrieked. "You didn't do anything at all! You forced her into a situation that was so awful she had no other choice but to make a drastic decision in order to escape. It's your fault she's being tortured right now. It's your fault that boy is dead."

Zoren let out a sharp crack of laughter, causing the lights to flicker.

"You expect me to believe that you are suffering here in the Underworld in your marriage to Prince Elijah? I am no fool, Chloe."

I shook my head. I was too angry to blush at the knowledge that even my father knew how fond Elijah and I had grown of each other. In his eyes, it was evidence that he made the right decision by arranging the marriages. The only reason Rose and Finn didn't work out was because there was something wrong with *her*.

"Elijah is nothing like Prince Finn," I snapped. "They are two completely different situations."

"Well, isn't that the truth," Zoren said with a cackle. "You are correct in saying that the younger prince is nothing like the firstborn heir. As such, he suits you."

He wrinkled his nose with distaste as he said the last sentence, indicating that it wasn't intended to be a compliment. Zoren was cruel to the point of risking pure stupidity. It wasn't wise of him to be insulting Prince Elijah and his wife in the palace of the God of the Underworld.

Yet, as he'd told me, he was the god of arts and literature, not the god of knowledge. If he were a wiser man, he never would've been tricked by the goddess of deceit in the first place.

But I was glad that he was. Every time that he had to face the God of the Underworld and learn that there was no progress in seeking out the trickster goddess, he had to face the embarrassment of his idiocy and carelessness. He, a minor god, had to grovel at the feet of a major god because he made a mistake and didn't have the strength to fix it on his own.

However, that knowledge was only somewhat satisfying. My father deserved his shame, but I was also beginning to think that my father deserved to be punished for his actions.

The events of that earlier that morning in Corruption were far from my mind as I stared down the god across the room, wishing that I was more than a mere demigoddess so that I could set him on fire with my eyes. It wouldn't kill him, but I had a feeling it would make me feel a little bit better.

"Leave," I hissed at him, pointing to the door. "Don't you have a lowly kingdom to win back?"

Zoren pursed his lips at me. "Ah, so you think you are better than me because of the social position I have arranged for you to achieve. No matter. I am not insulted by that. Although you seem to be convinced otherwise, I have always wanted the best for my daughters. In some ways, I think Tempest and her deceitful ways have given me a golden opportunity that I otherwise would not have had. You should be thanking me, Chloe. You have this life because of me."

I didn't know what to say. I was so outraged that I swore my vision was going red. If only my divine gifts were more than just the ability to read and study well. If only I was powerful like Elijah and could bless or curse an object. If only I was frightening like Finn and could command the respect of an entire room with one blink of my eyes.

If only I were like Nico, who was so alluring on the surface, but who harbored a dark volatility underneath it all.

If I were immortal, I would be able to do more than simply talk back to my father. I wouldn't have to stand there and listen to him gaslight me into being blindly grateful for him just because he happened to concoct a reasonable match between my prince and me.

"Leave," I repeated. "This is not your home. This is not your kingdom. *Leave.*"

Zoren tutted his tongue. "You are weak, Chloe. You think that spying on mischievous princes makes you brave, but it only makes you a fool. I am warning you once again to steer clear of Nico."

Part of me wanted to ask him if he knew something that I didn't. Why did Nico have bleeding human hearts on an altar? Who were those sacrifices for? Which god or goddess was the Lilith snake coercing him to pray to?

Of course, my father did not know the answers

to those questions. His motivations were not to ensure that Nico wouldn't hurt anyone but merely that he wouldn't get in the way of Zoren's daughters being successful in their marriages. If he was praying to a dark being, he clearly had other things on his mind than playing reverse matchmaker, so it was therefore of no further concern to my father.

He was selfish. He was a monster.

"I don't care what you think of me, Father," I told him, urging my voice to remain even and strong as I spoke. "I am not the weak one in this room, but that is an unimportant debate for us to have. I am Elijah's wife now. I am the princess of Disgrace. I have a throne and a kingdom of my own. If you can renounce your daughters, then I can renounce my father. That is what I choose to do."

"How dare you—"

"You have no power over me!" I shouted, taking another step toward him. The amusement melted from his gaze, replaced by raw disdain. "Go ahead and try to strike me down! I dare you! I am the daughter-in-law of the King of Hell, and one day I will be immortal in the Underworld. One day, I will have more power than you can ever manipulate for yourself. That is where you have failed, father. You believed that having powerful daughters in advantageous marriages would increase your power, but it has only revealed your weakness. It has only proven that you do not have the strength to stand on your own."

To his credit, Zoren looked surprised by my rant. Even I was taken aback by the ferocious vitriol in my voice. It was unlike me to speak so much in the first place, let alone with so much anger behind my words.

Suddenly, a knock on the door caused both of our heads to snap in the direction of the entrance.

"Ah," murmured Zoren, his tone difficult to decode. "I would rather not deal with two ungrateful daughters at once. I shall go now."

In confusion, I glanced back at my father, but he was already fading away into nothing but wisps of smoke. He knew who was knocking on my door already, but his statement made no sense.

Two ungrateful daughters? Which one of my sisters was paying me a visit now?

CHAPTER 14

When I opened the door and discovered who was standing on the other side, I almost slammed it shut again.

It was Riven, dressed in rich blue silk and wearing a subtle circlet of gold in her inky curls. If not for the sneer on her face, she would've looked every bit the picture of a perfect queen.

"What?" I snapped.

Riven snorted. "Hello to you, too. What's with the outfit? I wasn't aware I had a brother."

"That's hilarious," I quipped. "Are you sure you're not the daughter of the god of comedy?"

"You need to work on your comebacks."

"I'm not in the mood, Riven," I growled.

She smirked. "Clearly. I was just in the neighborhood, and I was sure I overheard the familiar sounds of a fight with father dearest. So kind of him to scram once he heard me knocking. I think he's afraid of me…"

"What do you want?" I sighed, one hand on the door and the other on the doorframe, effectively barring Riven from entering the room. I wanted to be alone. I wanted to sit in the quiet solitude of my study and write down thorough notes about everything I witnessed earlier with Nico, and then I wanted to curl up beside the fire and wait for Elijah to return with an update about Rose.

I did not want to play host to half my family.

"I'm surprised," Riven said, purposefully ignoring my question. "I thought I was the only one who dared to argue with him. I didn't expect you to be the only other daughter who has the guts to stand up to him."

"Why were you listening outside my door anyway?" I asked. "Your rooms aren't in this wing of the palace. You have no reason to be down this way unless you're so bored with your marriage that you feel the need to stalk me."

"Can I just please come in?" she snapped impatiently, craning her neck to see past my shoulder into the room. "Elijah is gone, isn't he? Can't you figure out how to keep your man entertained, Chloe? No wonder he runs off so early in the morning."

"You know, I never understand why you pair your requests with insults," I remarked. "Why would I want to invite you in if all you're going to do is make rude comments about a relationship you know nothing about?"

Riven rolled her eyes, but she deflated slightly. She wore a thick mask in front of the world. To all others but her sisters, she was charming and poised, and regal. When she only had me or one of our siblings to perform for, she was defensive and defiant, and ruthlessly insulting.

Who was she really, underneath all those carefully crafted personas?

"Fine," she sighed. "I'm sorry for the attitude. It's just that knowing father is near makes me feel agitated."

I snorted. She was making a poor excuse. If that was the case, Riven wouldn't be unpleasant all the time; which she was.

But still. I didn't blame her. I also wasn't a fan of our father, especially after the argument we just had. And at least she apologized, right?

Reluctantly, I stepped aside and let her into the reception room. She bustled in immediately, observing her surroundings with cool detachment.

"It's nice in here," she admitted as I shut the door and turned to face her expectantly. I couldn't begin to fathom what the purpose of her house call could be. Maybe she needed more help with the library but had to find a way to make my life miserable in the process. "Is this what the palace of Disgrace looks like?"

"Not really," I replied, taking in the ultra-luxurious interior decor that I still hadn't gotten used to yet. "Elijah and I have more humble taste."

"I would imagine," Riven said, her tone oddly neutral. I'd expected her to take the opportunity for another insult, but she must've been taking my statement about her mean streak to heart. "Why were you and father fighting anyway?"

I shrugged, watching as Riven plopped down into the armchair by the fire without invitation, kicking her feet up on the ottoman with casual disregard for formality.

"Why do *you* and father fight?" I countered.

Riven smirked. "You're clever. I always knew that, but I didn't know it translated to such witty evasiveness."

"Seriously, Riven. What do you want?"

In response, my sister's expression darkened. She tilted her head to the side and stared into the fire.

That's when I noticed that she was fidgeting.

Riven never fidgeted. She was the picture of poise, born with the ability to move as though she was always in the middle of a graceful dance. As I approached and sank down in the chair opposite her, Riven didn't glance up from the fire. There was something strange about her, but not like before when the Lilith snake was nearby. She didn't appear disturbed or have that faraway look in her eyes. Rather, the difference I noted was in her overall aura. She seemed tense and jumpy—somewhat unstable. As if she would crumble or explode or lash out if I prodded her in the wrong way.

"Rose deserves what she's going through," Riven murmured after a moment. She still did not remove her gaze from the fire, nor did she sound particularly convinced by the words coming out of her mouth. "She cheated on her fiancé and then ran away with her lover. She's always been too weak to realize when a great opportunity is staring her right in the face."

"Did you ever stop to think that maybe people don't want the same opportunities as you?" I snapped back, thinking of the lovely little cottage in the meadow that represented Rose's truest desires. "Just because their ambition is not aimed in the same direction as yours does not make them a lesser person."

Riven blinked, shifted slightly, then stared deep into my eyes.

"You and I are going to have to fundamentally disagree on that, sis," she replied. "We see the world in different ways. Do not endeavor to change my mind."

I was more stubborn than she thought. Everything about her frail composure told me that she was fighting a harsh inner battle. There seemed to be no other logical explanation for why she would seek me out in my private rooms unless she was desperate. Eager to nudge my sister in the general direction of redemption, I decided to tell Riven the truth.

"It's not true, you know," I told her. "Rose never cheated on Finn."

Riven raised a single eyebrow at me, wordlessly waiting for me to elaborate.

"Asher was her friend," I continued. "Just her friend. She cared for him because he was the only person in that palace who was kind to her—"

"Oh, please," scoffed Riven. "She acted like it was

such torture to be there. As if she were cursed by simply being engaged to one of the most powerful men in the world. No wonder she and Finn had no chemistry. She treated him like he was a demon."

I frowned at Riven in disapproval. Prince Finn was cold, cruel, and arrogant. He behaved as though he truly believed he was better than most other people. Personally, I didn't like being around him. I certainly wouldn't be thrilled by the prospect of having to marry him.

Rose was even softer than me. I imagined she saw Finn's superiority as a dark cloud hanging over her. Coupled with the reality that she didn't want to be a queen, let alone a queen in the Underworld, it was easy to understand why Rose sought out a friend who didn't make her feel so small and doomed. Surely, if Riven took one second to think about the situation from a perspective that wasn't her own, she could see that?

"Like I said," I hissed. "Not everyone has the same ambitions as you. Rose was unhappy, and she met a boy who made her feel happy, and then she escaped because he offered to help her. They were never lovers, Riven. He was just a kind person whose good heart became his downfall."

Riven glared at me. "How do you know that?"

I thought about lying, but then I figured there was no point in hiding the fact that I'd visited the darkest pits. If the God of the Underworld knew, what was the harm in Riven knowing?

"I visited her."

"You… what?"

"I went to the darkest pits with Elijah, and I spoke with her."

Riven stared at me, lips parted in surprise. "But, why?"

"That's where Elijah has been going every day," I explained. "He wanted to offer her comfort, being the prince of Disgrace. Everyone believes she's a disgraced woman. An adulteress."

"I don't understand," Riven muttered. I caught the gentlest tremor in her voice. I didn't think she'd have such a strong reaction to hearing that I went to see our sister. "Why didn't she argue her case?"

I ran my fingers through my hair, untangling the braid that I loosely tied up before leaving to follow Nico. In all fairness, I'd asked myself the same question.

"Have you ever had any luck arguing against a god?" I asked her.

Riven scoffed. "Fair point."

"And Rose is—bWell, she's not very argumentative, is she? She knew there was no point, so she did not try."

"And she let a boy die for her in the process," sneered Riven. "See? Rose is not the perfect little princess everyone used to think she was."

"At least she's capable of regretting the harm she has caused."

My words landed like knives. I could feel their sharpness as they dripped off my tongue, slicing through the air on their way to Riven.

She stood up instantly and glared down at me.

"You think I don't feel guilty for what I did to Prince Nico?" she yelled, looming over me. "Do you really think that I walk around this world without an ounce of remorse for the things I do to get ahead? That's life, Chloe. We make decisions, and then we have to live with them. Anyway, everything will be worth it when I meet my final goal."

"What is that, being Queen of Hell?" I replied.

Riven laughed humorlessly. "You really think that's all I want? Get a grip, Chloe. For someone who is so well-read, you're incredibly small-minded. Becoming queen is only a means to the end. But I'm not going to elaborate any further. You'll just have to wait and see."

Learning that Riven had some kind of diabolical

master plan was not comforting. However, I knew her ambition was strong. All I could do was hope that I was back in Disgrace, tucked far away in a peaceful corner of the Underworld, when she blew a blazing path to whatever her vague goal was. Whatever journey she was on, the Lilith snake would either help or hinder her.

I told myself that I didn't care if Riven was doomed. I told myself that it was better, in this instance, to see things the way she did. People made their beds and then had to have the courage to lie in them, according to her. Shouldn't she deserve a taste of her own medicine either way?

I didn't know what else to say to her, and then I was reminded that she still hadn't told me the reason for her visit.

As I opened my mouth to ask for her a third time, an odd expression suddenly took over her features. Her satisfied smirk melted into a weak grimace and her eyelids fluttered as if she was overcome by a random wave of exhaustion. Her body wavered slightly where she stood, and, for a moment, I wondered if I was going to have to reach out and catch her, but then she stepped backward and dropped back down into the chair.

She cleared her throat and smoothed down the

front of her skirts, already trying to build up her shields again and pretend that she didn't almost faint in front of me.

There was definitely something wrong with Riven. She was physically fit, strong, and sure on her feet. Never in my life had I seen her exhibit weakness like that. Was it the Lilith snake? Or was it something else entirely?

Taking advantage of her brief vulnerability, I decided to pry.

"Riven, why are you with your husband right now?" I asked.

Instinctively, I braced myself for her to bite back at me with something insulting, but she returned her gaze to the fire as a shiver caused her shoulders to shake gently.

A pained expression colored her gaze.

"It keeps telling me to go to him," she whispered. I leaned in, unsure if I was hearing her correctly. "That's the first thing it said to me. I don't think I was ever supposed to listen to it."

"What's *it*?" I asked, despite the fact that I was confident I already knew what she was talking about. Regardless of my determination not to feel bad for her, a flicker of concern glimmered inside me.

Riven shook her head quickly as if to dispel her own thoughts. She glared at me once again.

"Nothing," she hissed. "Forget it. I'm just tired from my future queen duties. I wouldn't expect you to understand."

Her insult didn't have the usual ferocity behind it. I could tell that she knew how obvious it made her defensiveness.

"Riven—"

"Mind your business, Chloe," she snapped.

For some reason, I was reminded of the day that Riven pushed me out of a tree in my father's apple orchard. She'd shown up out of nowhere, hanging gracefully from a branch while I balanced precariously on a limb with my book. She was bored, looking for a victim to bait. In the end, when I didn't bite, she gave up and shoved me to the ground.

My wrist broke, and she called me clumsy for it, making it seem as though it was entirely my fault for falling down when she pushed me. It was horrible of her, especially since we were only kids at the time, but I never mentioned it to anyone except my mother, who arranged for the divine doctor to mend my bones before my father could see that something was wrong with me.

Riven wanted me to mind my business, but the

truth was that I'd always done that. My whole life, keeping my head down and sticking my nose in a book instead of someone else's problems was the most effective way to keep myself out of trouble. And yet, even when I did everything I could to hide away and avoid misfortunes, Riven sought me out anyway.

Minding my business never got me very far, so I decided I was fed up with it. Instead of deigning to respond to Riven, I stood up and marched into the next room. She stayed where she was, but when I glanced over my shoulder, I saw that she was leaning over the edge of the armchair to watch me with a confused frown.

I fetched one of my notebooks from my desk in the study, the first one of many that the library had provided me with over the past week and brought it back to Riven. I thrust it out at her, leaving her no choice but to accept it.

She stared blankly at the cover. "What is this? Your diary?"

"Open it," I demanded, refusing to sit back down.

Riven rolled her eyes but did as she was told. As she absorbed the disorganized tangle of notes from my first few research attempts in the library, I noticed the crease between her brows grow deeper by the second.

"I don't understand," she told me, lifting her eyes and pursing her lips. She was lying.

I snatched the book from her and flipped the page that marked the moment I realized there was a Lilith snake following Riven around, thanks to Amalia's unexpected espionage report. I smoothed down the crease and then handed it back to her.

"The night of my wedding, when I saw you on the balcony, I knew something was wrong," I told her. "I'd never seen you act like that. I also noticed you acting weird during Rose's trial. As you can see, I haven't been very good at *minding my business* recently, and I have no intention of improving that behavior because clearly, you are hiding something from everyone."

"You're wrong—"

"Don't lie to me!" I shouted, raising my voice at my older sister for the first time in my life. "I know there's a Lilith snake targeting you. Is that what you meant just now? Did it lead you to Finn? Are you trying to tell me that the reason you aren't by his side right now is because you're afraid he's your doom? What a shame, Riven! You went to so much trouble to ensnare him!"

"He's not—"

"And I know you were researching snakes in the library the other day," I continued. "Don't even try to deny it. You played with fire, but now everything is burning around you. Have you figured out how to get rid of a Lilith snake yet? Do you even know how to get yourself out of this disaster? Or are you going to let it warp you into you're just a mindless tool for Lilith herself and lead *all* of us to our doom?"

"Finn is not—"

"And what about Nico?" I hissed before I could stop myself.

At the mention of her former lover, Riven paused in her attempts to interrupt me. My hesitation was also immediate.

Riven narrowed her eyes. "What about Nico? What do you mean?"

"H-he's not… himself," I replied lamely. So, Riven didn't know that Nico was likely also under the influence of a Lilith snake. They weren't caught up together in an evil scheme.

That wouldn't make sense if it were true, I reminded myself. Once Riven realized that she didn't have to settle for the second son, she wiped her hands clean of Nico.

Their dark paths were diverged, though equally shadowy.

Riven stood up, my journal still in her hands.

"I think I've had enough," she sighed. "And I think you should be careful what you get involved in, Chloe. This isn't a storybook. You can't escape the nightmares that happen in the real world."

Her words were chilling, but it was nothing compared to what she did next.

With a nasty sneer that marred her beautiful face, she tossed my journal into the hearth. Within seconds, it was consumed by flames. I stared at the smoldering pages and the smooth leather cover that I admired so much when the library offered it to me. All of the knowledge inside that journal was inside my head; I hadn't lost it just because Riven was burning it, but that wasn't her point.

She was warning me. She was denying my concern for her and trying to teach me a lesson, but nothing was more obvious to me at that moment than the plain fact that Riven did not throw my journal into the fire because she wanted to thwart me.

She did it because she was afraid. She was terrified of the truth scrawled on those pages. She didn't want the horrors to be real. Riven was making fun of my love of fiction because she didn't know how to express that she desperately wished her nightmares weren't real.

But Riven didn't want to be pitied. The longer we stared at each other in tense silence, the more she could tell that I wasn't angry at her but sad for her and the treacherous web she had woven.

"Stop looking at me like that," she barked.

"I don't—" I started to reply, but my protest was cut off by the sound of yet another knock on the door.

You've got to be kidding me.

CHAPTER 15

"Is there a sign on my door that reads *Come inside for untold riches and all your dreams come true?*" I grumbled aloud, stomping to the door.

However, before I could reach for the knob, it opened a few inches.

Milou, my maid from Disgrace, poked her head inside.

"I'm so sorry for the interruption, madam," she squeaked, eyes growing wide as she caught sight of who my visitor was. "It's just that your presence is being requested by his Majesty the God of the Underworld in the throne room. Both of you."

"Both of us?" Riven piped up from behind me.

Milou nodded nervously. "Yes. Apparently, it's rather urgent."

"Did he provide no other details?" Riven snapped at my maid. I shot her a venomous look.

"It's okay, Milou," I told her gently. "You don't have to answer her. Thank you for letting us know. We'll head down there right away."

Milou curtsied and scurried away, visibly shocked at the scene she had just witnessed. Even for a servant who worked her entire life in Disgrace and knew very little about the dynamic between the daughters of Zoren, she understood how strange it was for Riven to be in my rooms.

I glanced at Riven, the door still hanging open.

"What's this about?" I asked her.

She screwed up her face with a mocking expression. "How would I know? You think the God of the Underworld whispers all his secrets to me just because I'm his firstborn's wife?"

"Isn't that what you want anyway?" I bit back.

Riven rolled her eyes and forcefully shoved past me into the hallway.

"Come on," she called over her shoulder. "We don't want to keep our beloved father-in-law waiting."

All at once, she had changed her demeanor. The slight droop in her shoulders and dullness in her voice were gone. She spoke with a bright, cheerful voice, not an ounce of sarcasm in her statement about the God of the Underworld.

Another mask.

Reluctantly, I left my rooms and followed Riven down the hall toward the throne room. My introverted nature was screaming at me. I'd thought trailing Nico was the only thing I was going to have to deal with that day, and then I could relax by myself and recover in peace until Elijah returned from his visit with Rose in the pits. Instead, I'd played host to my father and my least favorite sister and was now being summoned by the King of Hell.

I wished there was a way I could get out of whatever this upcoming meeting was. I was desperate to write down everything I saw earlier that morning before I forgot the details. Plus, I really wanted to tell Elijah about the Lilith snake theories bouncing around inside my head. He would probably disapprove of me confronting Riven the way I did, but he didn't understand how difficult it was to approach things the normal and polite way when faced with someone like her.

Riven and I didn't speak the entire way down. I assumed she was stewing over our confrontation, full of festering regret that I managed to figure out so many of her secrets. I was so consumed with thoughts about her and Zoren and Nico that I couldn't spare an inch of mental storage to ponder the reason why the God of the Underworld wanted to talk to my sister and me.

When we descended the grand staircase into the all-too-familiar throne room, I saw that Amalia was already there. Dressed in her typical attire of a long, shapeless frock the color of pitch and her clunky boots, Amalia stood with her hands clasped politely in front of her in front of the God of the Underworld's throne.

"Hello, girls!" the god greeted Riven and me. "My darlings, you look beautiful as always. Riven, that shade suits your skin tone flawlessly, and Chloe, I must admit that you look wonderful in those trousers."

We nodded our heads in thanks, dipping into curtsies when we reached the base of the dais on which the God of the Underworld's throne rested. He was in an uncharacteristically cheerful mood. Downright gleeful, if I had to describe his giddy smile and twinkling eyes. For some reason, I found myself thinking that it was a bad sign for the god to be in such pleasant spirits. The kind of things that brought the King of Hell joy were naturally not the same things that I would also be happy about.

Still, I reminded myself that he was, indeed, my father-in-law, and being anything other than perfectly polite would risk Elijah's relationship with his father. Not to mention, it might endanger future visits to the darkest pits of Hell for both me and Elijah, which would only harm Rose.

So, instead of revealing my true feelings about the God of the Underworld, I kept my face serene, calm, and patient.

Unfortunately, Riven beat me to the punch.

"Your Majesty, I thought we wouldn't get the delight of your company until dinner this evening," she chirped from beside me. "What a lovely surprise!"

The God of the Underworld chortled like a jolly old man, endeared by Riven's faux flattery. It was annoying that he couldn't see right through her. Because I'd known her for my entire life, all I could think about was how obvious her sucking up was.

I glanced at Amalia, who was already gazing at me with her spooky gray eyes. She offered me a knowing glance as if she wanted to tell me something, just like the way she did when she appeared in the library. Before I decoded the hidden message in her gaze, two sets of footsteps echoed on the staircase behind us.

"Here are the little ones!" exclaimed the God of the Underworld.

The three of us turned to find Danai and Sasha descending the staircase with ill-disguised confusion but an appropriate amount of passivity, nonetheless. They knew better than to look disgruntled in front of the god, even if they had been yanked out of whatever they were doing to come down the throne room.

When the five of us were gathered together beneath his throne, the God of the Underworld clapped his hands together in a praying gesture and smiled at each of us.

"Now that you're all here, I wanted to announce some very good news," he began. So, this was it. He only wanted to speak to the five of us. That last time we were all standing in front of him like this, it was the day of Rose and Finn's wedding, and we were learning for the first time that she had disappeared. As such, I couldn't blame myself for the uncomfortable sense of unease sinking into my limbs.

"Of course, I suppose it would make the most sense for me to announce this to everyone all at once at our family dinner tonight, but I felt it was important for you girls to hear about it first," he said, each word he uttered only leaving me more puzzled.

"Now, I want you to meet someone. Come on out, love!"

A servant opened the door to the left of the god's throne, and a girl emerged from within. She was beautiful, wearing a demure smile on her porcelain-doll face as she stepped forward and faced the five of us. She looked to be about mine or Riven's age and stood taller than me but shorter than Riven, with slender limbs and pristine posture. The girl had thick hair left to hang in effortless waves around her shoulders and green eyes that were so bright they seemed unnatural. Overall, despite her prettiness, the effect was somewhat off-putting. Perhaps it was stupid, but the girl seemed *too* perfect as if she was nothing more than a mirage.

"Girls," the God of the Underworld said, admiring the strange girl with warm affection in his eyes. "I would like you to meet Circe, your fellow demigoddess. She is the daughter of Eliana, minor goddess of weaving."

Goddess of weaving? *Weaving?* There was a goddess for that? That was worse than being the daughter of the god of arts and literature.

Still, the God of the Underworld appeared undeniably fond of her.

Circe smiled at us and curtsied with enviable

precision as if she'd spent the past decade of her life practicing how to perform royal manners and nothing else.

"I'm very pleased to make your acquaintance, demigoddesses."

We curtsied in response, though Riven and I were dipping into more shallow bows than our sisters because of our higher rank as proper princesses of the Underworld. Childishly, I thought how annoying it was to have to share something like that with her. I hated to have something in common with my infuriating older sister.

"Circe is going to be a guest at the palace for the next year, just like you five ladies," said the God of the Underworld. "Please do your best to make her feel welcome and to help her become familiar with the palace. She has traveled a long way. I expect kindness as you welcome her into your hearts, as she will become your sister—for lack of a better word— very soon."

Clearly, the God of the Underworld could see the shock and confusion written on all of our faces. I glanced between him and Circe, then attempted to sneak a look at Riven, but her face was angled away from me, and I couldn't read her expression. However, if I could read her mind, I knew I would hear her sizing the exquisite girl up and doing quick calculations to determine as many of her weaknesses as possible.

Meanwhile, my brain was sluggishly churning to put all the pieces of information together. It was tired and stuffed with too much information; I didn't know how many more surprises I could handle.

Thankfully, that was when the God of the Underworld decided to cut to the chase.

"I know you have all been wondering—and, in fact, all of the Underworld has been wondering, as well—how the search for a new betrothal for my second born Prince Nico has been going," he said, grinning from ear to ear. "I'm so pleased to tell you that, much like yourselves, we have found a wonderful match in the most unlikely of places! Of course, Nico and Circe have already become acquainted, but you five girls are the only other people currently privy to this exciting news!"

Of course. How did I not catch on right away? Obviously, the young, beautiful demigoddess was here to marry Prince Nico, who was forced back into the single life when Riven exchanged him for an upgrade. She looked nice enough; her smile was genuine and bright, at least. Still, there was something about her that didn't seem right. Maybe I was being too judgmental. Or maybe my brain was still in paranoia mode after the day I'd had.

Gods and it wasn't even noon.

I waited for Riven to say something. Since the beginning, she had been the one to speak up when the rest of us were stuck in polite silence. She played the apologetic diplomat when Rose ran away, she did most of the talking at the dinner table out of us, and she presumably had plenty of other personal meetings with the God of the Underworld in the lead up to her marriage to his firstborn.

However, for the first time, Riven was silent.

A slight awkwardness settled over the room as my younger sister shuffled their feet and mumbled half-hearted *hellos* to Circe and her shiny emerald eyes.

I wondered what Riven was thinking. Here was the girl that was chosen to replace her. Did she feel jealous? It wasn't fair of her, but that didn't mean it wasn't possible. At one point, Riven and Nico were openly affectionate with each other. I'd even bet that they'd been intimate with one another long before it ever became a possibility that Rose and Finn weren't going to work out, thus shaking things up.

Do you think I don't feel guilty for what I did to Prince Nico?

Riven's words suddenly took on a different meaning. Deep down, did she still have feelings for him? If she knew what he was up to while he snuck away to Corruption, would she still not change her heart?

Or perhaps Riven's silence was stoic disapproval. Perhaps she had already decided that she didn't like Circe and that, as Nico's former partner, her opinion on the matter of his next partner was important.

Overall, there was no reason for Riven to feel threatened. She was already married to Prince Finn and clearly fond of him if she was willing to argue that he was *not* her doom, despite being led to him by the Lilith snake. It wasn't like Circe could unravel their marriage at this point.

As I tried to think of all the possible paths of paranoia my older sister was mentally running down, I noticed that the God of the Underworld's smile was fading as the silence stretched on. If someone didn't say something charming and enlightened soon, he was going to get upset.

And, for my younger sisters' sakes, the last thing I wanted was for the god to favor his shiny, new future daughter-in-law over the rest of us. If Riven was short-circuiting, I supposed the responsibility of graceful politeness would fall on the shoulders of the third daughter of Zoren.

I stepped forward and said the first thing that came to mind.

"It's nice to meet you, Circe," I said, loud and clear as I offered her a warm smile. "Welcome to the Underworld. Now, forgive me if you get this question often but, as the daughter of the goddess of weaving, I am wondering if you're skilled at braiding hair? If so, I would love to learn from you."

As I spoke, I comically pointed to the pathetic remnants of my leftover braid from this morning. Much to my relief, the God of the Underworld chuckled.

Circe grinned, visibly consoled by my kindness. She, too, was growing anxious in the prolonged quiet that followed her introduction.

"Unfortunately, I am quite bad at braiding," she admitted humbly. "However, I am gifted with the loom, and I adore your trousers. Would you mind if I made a pair just like them for myself?"

It was the third comment I'd received about the fact that I was wearing pants. If only they knew that the only reason I'd donned the ensemble was to efficiently spy on Circe's new fiancé.

But that was a secret that would stay between Elijah and me.

I nodded at Circe. "Of course. I'm flattered to be a source of inspiration."

Still, Riven did not speak. It was downright uncharacteristic of her not to be demanding the spotlight, especially with fresh meat being tossed into the equation. Unbearably baffled by her silence, I turned to offer her a questioning look, only to find that Riven was white as a sheet.

She was staring at Circe as if she was not seeing a girl but a ghost.

It wasn't the first time I'd seen that look on her face.

My breath caught in my throat as Riven began to tremble.

"Riven," I whispered, taking a step toward her.

But before I could reach out to her, Riven's coal-black eyes rolled back into her head, and she collapsed on the cold floor at my feet.

Sign up for the newsletter to be notified of new releases.

All of Rye's Books

Sign up for the newsletter to be notified when it's released.
Click on link for
Newsletter
or put this in your browser window:
mailerlite.com/webforms/landing/k9z2k8